SEARCH AND RESCUE

A *Just Cause Universe* Novel

IAN THOMAS HEALY

Local Hero Press Edition

Search and Rescue
Published by Local Hero Press, LLC
http://localheropress.com

1st Printing
Local Hero Press: trade paperback, June 11, 2019
Printed in the United States of America

ISBN-13: 9781971445151

Cover art by Chaz Kemp
Book design by Local Hero Press, LLC

Books by Local Hero Press

Author Notes

I've wanted to write this story for a long time, but it took me until late 2018 to really firm up the concept. I didn't have a central character in mind, didn't have a plot hook. All I knew was I wanted to tell a tale set in the Arctic.

I've never been to the Arctic myself; I'm a lover of desert climate. I recognize the stark beauty in the far north, and how climate change is transforming it. It only makes sense that in the setting of the Just Cause Universe, a team would be established to police the top of the world. As we see more evidence of climate change firsthand in the form of extreme weather, even the Arctic can't go untouched, and hurricane-like Arctic cyclones are a real thing. What better setting for a team optimized for search and rescue operations than to put them in the middle of a terrible storm? And then, of course, I turned everything on its ear.

Like all *Just Cause Universe* books, this one can be read as a standalone. Without spoiling anything, situations and characters referenced in this book have been in previous books in the series, and the events in *Search and Rescue* will have consequences in future books. I'm playing the long game here (*Very* long – *Search and Rescue* is the 16th book in a series that began in 2003 and will be continuing for at least a few more years).

No book can reach publication without the help of a team of superheroes, and I've got several I need to thank here. My beta readers Adrienne Dellwo, Chris Preyor, and Ira Creasman have worked hard to make this a better book than what I originally sent to them. I couldn't have done it without their help. I'm especially grateful to artist Chaz Kemp, who stepped in to do a fantastic cover. My family, as always, is ridiculously supportive of this crazy writing business. Finally, I want to thank you, the fans, who keep coming back for more of the *Just Cause Universe*. As long as I have more stories to tell, and you keep reading them, I promise to keep writing them.

- Ian Thomas Healy
May, 2019

If you want to listen to the music Maia listens to during this book, here is a consolidated playlist:

Maia's Playlist

"Does Anybody Really Know What Time It Is?" - Chicago
"Top of the World" - The Carpenters
"I Am the Walrus" - The Beatles
"The Wind Cries Mary" - The Jimi Hendrix Experience
"Ship of Fools" - Grateful Dead
"Always Crashing in the Same Car" - David Bowie
"Dust in the Wind" - Kansas
"Jump Into the Fire" - Harry Nilsson
"Burn / Stormbringer" - Whitesnake
"Flaming Telepaths" - Blue Öyster Cult
"Stand and Fight" - James Taylor
"Hall of the Mountain King" - Rainbow
"All Cats Are Grey" - The Cure
"We Are the Dead" - David Bowie
"Electric" - The Church
"Secrets" - Tears for Fears
"Red Right Hand" - Nick Cave & The Bad Seeds
"Going, Going, Gone" - Bob Dylan
"Monster / Suicide / America" - Steppenwolf
"Edge of the Ocean" - Ivy
"Voices in the Sky" - The Moody Blues
"Walking on the Moon" - The Police
"The Battle Rages On" - Deep Purple
"The Killing Moon" - Echo and the Bunnymen
"War Pigs" - Black Sabbath
"Long Walk Home" - Bruce Springsteen
"Shadowplay" - Joy Division
"The Ocean" - Led Zeppelin
"Home by the Sea" - Genesis

Dedicated to Stan Lee, one of the world's true superheroes, gone but never forgotten.

Chapter One

From Maia's playlist: "Does Anybody Really Know What Time It Is?" - Chicago

June, 2020

Maia Young sat on a folding chair at one side of the stage and tried very hard not to throw up. The lights were too bright, the auditorium too hot, and her robe was making her skin itch. The gallery was full of people —instructors and younger students, current heroes and retired, families and friends. Factions within the audience cheered as names were read off, and Maia felt a little ill. She only had two people down among those seats, and she barely knew them at all.

"Rhiannon Adkins, known as Cacophony, has been accepted onto Just Cause New York," announced Keith Jordan, the hero formerly known as MetalBlade and the principal of the Hero Academy. Cheers and applause rang through the auditorium as Rhiannon gave the gallery a broad smile and stood. She had done all their makeup, of course, like she did for every public event. It wasn't a parahuman powers, but she was really good at it. Over the past couple years of experimenting, she'd even found a unique blend of greens, purples, and grays that accented Maia's naturally blue skin

Ingrid Jordan, also known as Icebreaker, Dean of Students, and Keith's wife, had a faint bluish tint to her skin as well, but she could pass for Caucasian in all but the brightest light. Nobody could mistake Maia for looking normal with her bulging muscles, pointed ears, and skin nearly the same color as a summer sky. Ingrid handed Rhiannon her diploma and shook her hand.

"Jacob Cotton, known as Calamity, has been accepted onto Just Cause Dallas."

Jacob got a lot of cheering, as he had a large family and had just helped to take down a dangerous supervillain the previous month. He'd been acting as a superhero even before attending the Hero Academy, having saved children from a flooding daycare in his hometown. He had always been nice to Maia, and she thought she would miss him more than most of the others in her class. She'd started half a year later than the rest of them, thanks to her previous set of foster parents—the Stanwycks—keeping her locked away because of her unusual appearance. Jacob had helped her with her schoolwork so she could catch up and graduate with the others her age.

"Lindsay Malone, known as Fireball, has been accepted onto Just Cause Los Angeles." Lindsay's mom was the assistant warden at Deep Six, the prison for parahuman criminals. More than once, the Stanwycks had threatened to send her there if she acted up, or tried to run away, or did anything they felt was immoral. They were religious fundamentalists, and they had told Maia her appearance was God's curse upon her. She knew better now, but the constant belittling and bullying had left a lasting skittishness. She'd been seeing the Academy's psychologist weekly since first starting, and although she knew she'd made progress in therapy, it was, as Dr. Kuramoto said, an ongoing process.

"L.J. Vincent, known as DaVinci, has been accepted onto Just Cause Richmond." L.J. was an odd young man with unusual powers. He, more than anybody, had been completely accepting of Maia when her new fosters, the Youngs, first brought her to the Hero Academy. He knew what it was like to be different, as he had a prosthetic leg and his powers didn't fall into any easily-classifiable category. He stood, winked back at Maia, and strode across the stage. In three years, she'd never learned what his initials stood for; neither had anyone else.

"You okay?" Chloe whispered to Maia. She was Maia's closest friend at school. Like Maia, her body had physically changed as her powers had matured. She'd grown gorgeous, functional dragonfly wings and overcome the social and personal challenges of being physically different with poise and grace that Maia envied.

Maia nodded, although she wasn't feeling okay. "I'm just . . . I hate being in the spotlight."

"You're going to be on Just Cause, Maia. It kind of comes with the territory. Whoops, here I go!" She grinned at Maia, who couldn't help but smile back.

"Chloe Wyld, known as WyldWing, has been accepted onto Just Cause Seattle." Thunderous cheering and applause filled the auditorium as Chloe stood to accept her diploma. In her four years at the Academy, she had probably saved more lives than many heroes did in their entire careers. From stopping an attack on the Academy itself to battling white supremacists in Idaho to helping Jacob stop a supervillain in Colorado, she had done more even than legendary Hero Academy graduate Mustang Sally. Maia figured Chloe would have an amazing career, and counted herself fortunate to have met her.

To Maia's left, Ava reached over and squeezed her hand. Ava was super-strong, like Maia, and had been her workout buddy during a lot of training. "Don't worry, Maia. You're going to do great."

Principal Jordan smiled over at Maia. "Maia Young, known as DevilFish, has been accepted onto Just Cause Arctic Circle." The applause from the gallery was polite and restrained except for Peter and Kristin Young, who cheered loudly for her. When she'd been removed from her first foster home, she'd wound up with them, and she had counted her blessings every day since. Where the Stanwycks had been cruel, the Youngs had been kind. Her former fosters hadn't given her hardly anything, the Youngs gave her their name, their knowledge, and their love. Maia hadn't even known people could be so caring and without judgment. Even though she'd spent most of the past three and a half years at the Academy, they'd never hesitated to send her care packages, to spend time with her when she was home for holidays, and to be the sort of parents she'd never known growing up.

Feeling like her head was in the fog, Maia accepted her diploma and handshakes from both of the Jordans, then went to stand beside Chloe on the opposite end of the stage. Chloe grabbed her hand, lending her strength. "We did it, Maia, we made it!"

"And finally, Ava Zhang, known as Flint, has been accepted onto Just Cause Chicago." Ava, who had somewhat of a dour personality, looked positively bubbly as she took her own diploma and skipped across the stage to join the others. Principal Jordan looked out at the gallery and held his hand out as if encompassing the eight young heroes to his right. "Friends, families, and assembled guests, I present to you your 2020 graduating class!"

Earsplitting applause and cheers erupted throughout the auditorium as the eight young heroes gleefully hurled their mortarboards into the rafters.

* * *

At the reception, the instructors all took time to wish the students the best, offering tidbits of advice over hors d'ouvres and beverages and a live DJ playing popular party music. Maia spent most of the time near the edge, sitting with her foster parents, who understood her need to be away from the center of attention. She wished the DJ would play more classic rock music, which was her favorite.

When she was growing up with the Stanwycks Maia wasn't allowed to listen to any music except hymns. That didn't mean she didn't ever hear other music; she just had to be sneaky about it. There was a boy who lived across the street. She didn't even know his name until she was twelve. It was Mason, and he was the most interesting person she knew as a child. He was several years older than her—how many, she didn't know, because her foster parents never spoke about him. He did yard work out front of the yellow house with an old-fashioned push mower in the summers and raking leaves around the trees in the fall. Most of the time, he did so in apparent silence thanks to his earbuds. She watched him when he was outside, because she secretly thought he was beautiful, and she knew nobody would ever think of her that way.

Sometimes, though, he would turn on his phone speaker and then Maia would get to hear Mason's music. It was barely audible a lot of the time, but it was there, and it was so *different* from the recordings the Stanwycks would play in the infrequent times when they chose music over grim silence. For one thing, Mason's music had real rhythm to it—strong beats that made Maia want to move, to *dance*, if such a thing were permitted. For another, so many of the songs were about love, about doing things that felt good, about seeking the enjoyment of life. Who wouldn't want that? And finally, of course, it never ever mentioned God.

A couple instructors stopped by to check in on Maia, wish her luck at her new posting. Like all the graduating seniors, she would start out as an intern at her assigned team, learning the ropes of the Just Cause organization in general and the needs of the assigned team in specific. They said she'd be an outstanding hero.

Maia didn't feel much like a hero. She missed half her freshman year at the Academy because of the time she spent learning how to live with her powers in a setting where she wasn't abused. The Youngs, who were teachers themselves, helped her understand them and how they worked, and even set up scientific experiments to help test those powers. She made up her missed hours the following summer, staying on campus so she could focus on her studies instead of returning to another foster home. Despite lacking a basic educational background thanks to poor-quality homeschooling, she buckled down and worked hard to maintain what were, at best, average academic grades. In the end, though, she got to graduate with the rest of her class, and when internships were assigned, she'd drawn the Frozen Wasteland, otherwise known as the fledgling Just Cause Arctic Circle.

JCAC was the newest team in the ever-growing organization, only a year old. As climate change cleared more and more sea ice during the summer months, more ships took the northern passages between the Pacific and Atlantic instead of traveling either through the Panama Canal or going all the way south around the tip of Tierra del Fuego. Based in Deadhorse, Alaska, the team was established to provide parahuman support for that increased traffic in the Arctic Ocean. JCAC focused on search and rescue instead of offensive capability. Sure, every member of Just Cause went through combat training, either at the Hero Academy or in the field, but nobody seriously expected a need for it in the Frozen Wasteland.

That suited Maia just fine, for she had shown a tendency to freeze from fear and indecision in combat training, and she was convinced her destiny lay with the Champions instead of Just Cause. The Champions were the minor leagues, where parahuman heroes went whose powers weren't up to snuff, or whose psychological makeup put them at odds with the Just Cause philosophy. Being a Champion didn't mean you were a failure. It just meant that for whatever reason, you weren't a good fit for Just Cause.

Maia, apparently, was a good fit after all.

Mustang Sally stopped by Maia's table with her family. The student rumor mill always operated at peak efficiency, so everybody knew Sally wasn't married to the father of her children, which Maia thought was especially scandalous given her upbringing. He was a tall, lean black man named March who spoke little due to a pervasive stutter. He had a nice smile, though, and the attraction between him and Sally was plain for anyone to see. Sally was the Academy's combat instructor, and she'd spent a lot of extra time working with Maia on evenings and weekends, trying to get the timid super-strong girl to overcome her combat paralysis, with limited success. Maia had been certain she was destined to be a Champion, but Sally herself had recommended her for the Arctic Circle team.

"March, try to keep the kids from terrorizing the party. I want to chat with Maia for a minute," Sally said.

March nodded, bent to kiss Sally's cheek, and headed off after their two-year-old twins Jason and Regina.

Sally turned to Maia. "How are you doing?"

Maia shrugged. "Everyone keeps asking me that."

"It's because we care, Maia. I wanted you to know I recommended you for the Frozen Wasteland. I think you'll do very well up there."

"I guess so."

"Despite your strength and toughness, you're never going to be a frontline fighter, and that's a hundred percent okay. There are hundreds of bricks and tanks out there who will gladly throw a punch given the chance, but your skills fall in other areas." Sally smiled. "I believe in you, Maia, and you can trust me. I'm never wrong about these sorts of things."

"I'll try not to disappoint anyone."

Sally leaned in close. "Want to know a secret? Nobody is going to be harder on you than you are on yourself. You're eighteen years old. Give yourself some time to figure things out. And give yourself time to live your life. Sometimes we get so caught up in being superheroes that we forget to be human beings." The pitter-patter of super-speedy toddler feet sounded like a drum roll as Sally's twins raced past and she lunged for them just as quickly, snagging her son and daughter into a hug. "Hey, you two. Where's your dad?"

"Slow, Momma," little Jason shouted with a laugh.

"Slow," Regina repeated. "He gonna Moon."

Sally laughed. "Well, I'm sure he's got a good reason for that. We'll go watch him leave." She turned to Maia, looking past her struggling twins. "I've got to handle these little monsters. Good luck in the Arctic, Maia. I know you'll do fantastic."

"Thanks, Ms. Tibbets."

"You've earned the right to call me Sally." She took her kids' hands. "Come on, you two. Let's go say goodbye."

* * *

The flight from Denver to Fairbanks was a grueling ten-hour journey with a brief respite of a layover in Seattle. Maia got to spend the first leg of the trip with Chloe on the way to her own internship at Just Cause Seattle. Neither Chloe nor Maia would fit in standard airline seats, Chloe because of her wings and Maia because of her size. It meant they got to fly first class. The two girls enjoyed the opportunity to stretch their legs and the perks of premium treatment by the flight crew, knowing it was likely the last time they would get to once they began their duties with Just Cause.

Although the Stanwycks claimed she'd been cursed by God, Maia now knew her body was the result of rampant genetic mutation, turning her from a slight, pale child with thin hair to what she'd become: grossly overmuscled and hairless from head to toe. Around the same time she started her monthly cycle, she awakened every night groaning in pain as her body heaped muscle upon even more layers of muscle. All her hair fell out, like she was the victim of some horrible disease, showing that her ears had pointed tips like some fantasy creature. And on top of everything, she turned *blue*. It had taken most of a year, so gradual that she didn't really notice the changes from day to day. Then one day she'd overheard the Stanwycks discussing it, and when she held her hand up against the porcelain tiles of the bathtub, there was no mistaking the distinctive bluish cast to her skin. It was the blue of a long-faded tattoo, of a ballpoint pen nearing the end of its ink reservoir. Now, at eighteen, her skin had darkened to a saturated sky blue.

Just Cause medical staff determined Maia had an insulating, super-dense fat sheath like whale blubber lining her entire body. When combined with her exceptional strength, size, and ability to hold her breath for half an hour, a whale-themed hero name seemed only logical. Gray whales had once been called *Devilfish*, and that sounded a lot neater than *Beluga*, which was the only other name she'd managed to suggest. Luckily, Just Cause had its own image consultant team, and they scrapped *Beluga* right away. They entertained several other nautical-themed names and costume designs, and Maia was enamored with *Orca*, only to learn that four different heroes and one criminal around the world already used the name. Devilfish was unique, and, as the chipper young woman with the big round glasses had said to her, unique was what Just Cause wanted in its heroes.

Her primary training at the Academy focused on her swimming skill, using her strength and breath-holding to enhance her movement in the water. She would never be an underwater speedster, but she could swim as fast as a speedboat, using her strength to pull herself through the water and special webbed gloves and soft boots that allowed her to dig through it even harder. Her layer of blubber kept her body temperature up even in ice-cold settings, and it was clear she would be at her best in that environment. She learned to love spending time in the water, exploring the bottoms of lakes and reservoirs near the Academy.

All that was great, but the more time she spent in the water, the less she felt at home on the land. She hadn't yet swum in the ocean, but got to dive in the Gulf of Mexico for her spring break trip as a senior. It had been the most amazing experience ever. She spent hours in the deep and felt her stresses melt away with every submersion. It wasn't just her growing love for the vast blue expanses, but she always felt awkward around other people, and it was easier to be alone below the surface.

By the time she finished her pubescent growth spurt, Maia was a head taller than Mr. Stanwyck, who himself was not a small man. She had huge slabs of muscle in her arms, legs, back, and chest. They were powerful, too. She sneaked into the garage one night when the Stanwycks were asleep and found she could lift the heaviest thing she knew—the car—with no trouble at all. All that gross musculature made her look overweight. The Stanwycks said she ate too much, when sometimes it felt like they barely fed her at all. They said her curse was making her fat, and they tried to starve her. She was hungry all the time—so much that it hurt. She would lie awake in her bedroom at night, silent tears of pain running down her cheeks after only getting a single piece of toast or a small bowl of bland, overcooked vegetables for a pathetic dinner.

Her stomach rumbled. Maybe she should find something to eat in the airport. It wasn't like she had to sneak food any longer. She could eat whenever she felt like it. When the Stanwycks slept, she would creep downstairs, having learned which steps and floorboards had to be avoided lest a creak give her away, and she'd steal food. She couldn't take much, because then her fosters would know. They inventoried the food before they left for church. They weren't so thorough that they weighed jars of peanut butter or counted slices of bread, but if she ate more than a bare minimum of anything, they would likely know and she would be punished. A mouthful of casserole here, a piece of bread there—anything to drive away the hunger pains without giving herself away.

Then had come the night she'd been found out. Mr. Stanwyck surprised her in the kitchen, catching her in the act of eating a folded-over peanut butter sandwich on a single piece of bread. "Thief!" he shouted. "Thou shalt not steal!"

He went to fetch his belt.

Maia had been beaten before. After her body changed, it didn't hurt anymore, but she didn't let her fosters know so they wouldn't find a worse way to punish her. Being beaten hurt in other ways, and even the thought of it brought tears of humiliation to her eyes. That night, she'd come to a decision that she wasn't going to be beaten anymore. She knew it was wrong, even though Proverbs 23:13 said not to withhold discipline from a child. There were other verses where Jesus spoke of love and kindness, and she liked those much better. When Stanwyck came after her with the belt, ready to administer yet another beating to the monster that was his ward, she ran.

It was the middle of the night when she crashed through the front door of the house and into the street. Sudden light shone from the upper floor of the yellow house and she saw Mason—who mowed lawns and listened to music—stare down at her from his bedroom window. "Help me!" she cried. Stanwyck tried to drag her back into the house, but she lowered her head and hunched down, resisting. She was strong enough that she could have dragged him away instead, if she'd wanted. She screamed for help again and more lights came on in houses on the block. Then came the neighbors, asking what was going on and warning Stanwyck to stop his abuse.

Abuse.

Maia hadn't known the word before that night, but she knew it now. She had been abused, neglected, all by people who were using the shield of their religion to justify it. Mason's parents called the police, who in turn called Social Services. While she waited, Maia sat in Mason's kitchen, wrapped in Mason's mother's bathrobe, eating a grilled cheese sandwich and tomato soup his mother made for her. It was the most delicious thing she'd ever had. When Social Services arrived, they removed Maia from the house which she'd called home since she was a toddler.

"Hey, Earth to Maia." Chloe snapped her fingers in front of Maia's face. "Did you hear me?"

"No, sorry." Maia shrugged, pulled out an earbud, and paused her music. Paul Simon would have to wait. "What'd you say?"

"I asked if you wanted me to wait with you during your layover. I can. I don't mind. It's only a thirty minute flight for me to get to Seattle HQ, and I don't have to wait for a car or anything." She buzzed her wings for emphasis.

"No, it's only a couple of hours, yeah?" Maia said. "I can watch a movie on my phone or listen to my music or something." A passerby in the concourse glanced at her, and then did a double take as he saw her less-than-human features. She pulled her lightweight hoodie a little further forward to better hide her broad, blue face. She wished she looked more like Chloe with her slender, athletic build, her delicate and pretty features, and her *hair*. She'd thought about wearing a wig, but the few she'd tried on made her look even stranger, so she eschewed them altogether.

"Are you okay?" Chloe was perceptive and sensitive to the discomfort of others.

"Yes. I'm just tired. Traveling is . . . rough," Maia lied. She knew Chloe would know she was lying, but would be polite enough not to call her out for it. Traveling *was* rough, but the truth was Maia was afraid. She didn't know what to expect on her new team. She'd had a hard time adjusting to all the new people at the Academy, and now she was going to have to do it all over again. Alaska was so far away from everything and everyone, and, well, it was a new experience and those always made her uncomfortable. At times like that, she tended to withdraw. When she was younger, she found solace in prayer, but she no longer felt like it was the answer. Praying hadn't stopped the Stanwycks' abuse. She knew God was supposed to help those who helped themselves, but the more she'd thought about it, she realized that those who helped themselves didn't *need* God's help. Instead, she listened to her music, and found solace in that.

Nevertheless, Chloe knew her well enough to know what she needed was someone who cared. The winged girl embraced her tightly, having to stand on her tiptoes to do so. "Hey, I'm going to miss you, Maia. Message me when you get to Deadhorse. Make sure you Instagram it."

"I will," Maia said.

Chloe departed, garnering a lot of attention as she flew over the other travelers, swinging her carry-on bag from one hand. An airport security guard hollered after her and she called back, "Sorry! Byeeee . . ." and disappeared down the concourse. Maia wandered over to a quiet spot by the gate for her connecting flight. She looked askance at the hard plastic seats, decided they would be too small and too uncomfortable, and instead sat on the carpeted floor with her back against a support pillar. She slipped her earbuds in and turned on her favorite playlist of classic rock. For the next two hours, she simply waited and enjoyed the music.

Chapter Two

From Maia's playlist: "Top of the World" - The Carpenters

The plane to Fairbanks was packed full of people, proof that Alaska was a popular tourist destination in the summertime. Maia still rode in first class, but she kept her hood pulled forward and didn't speak to any of the other travelers. She dozed on and off during the flight, awakening to the bump of the plane touching down in Fairbanks. Even though it had been morning when she and Chloe left Denver, the sun was still high in the sky, and she knew it wasn't going to set anytime soon once she went above the Arctic Circle. For the rest of the summer, the sun would be her constant companion.

Her connecting flight from Fairbanks to the north was a much smaller plane than the previous two. It had actual propellers and the flight attendants spent time moving people around inside the plane prior to takeoff, presumably to make sure the weight was balanced appropriately. Because of her size and inability to fit in the regular seats, Maia wound up in the tail by herself, which suited her just fine. The rest of the plane was filled with oilfield workers heading to Deadhorse for their next one- or two-week stretch at Prudhoe Bay. Some of them talked to each other but the drone of the propellers made conversation difficult, and mostly everyone just listened to their phones via noise-canceling headphones or earbuds like Maia did.

Maia let the music of the Carpenters drown out the noise of the engines as the plane took off. She looked down at Alaska as it passed beneath her and wondered what to expect. The plane flew over mountain ranges, sharp like the shattered bones of some ancient titan. Their course followed the Dalton Highway below, a winding gray ribbon of gravel road that carried lots of trucks and not much else. It was flyover country in every sense of the word.

Eventually the mountains flattened and became wide plains of snowfields dotted with islands of brown and green where it had melted. Some swaths were more bog than snow, with ponds everywhere. Maia saw a herd of caribou wandering through one patch and shivered. It was the first time she felt the distance between her and the rest of the world. At least the caribou belonged down there. She would be the alien, a stranger trying to fit in.

The plane touched down in Deadhorse. When the pilot informed them they could once again use their electronic devices, Maia texted Chloe to let her know she'd arrived.

Yay! was her friend's brief response, followed by a sleepy-dog GIF. Maia's phone had automatically updated to local time and she wondered if she'd just awakened Chloe. She promised to check in later once she'd gotten settled in and put away her phone.

Instead of taxiing to a jetway, a stairway truck rolled up to the jet and Maia descended onto the tarmac with the other passengers. The air was crisp but not chilling, and a gentle breeze carried away the worst stink of airplane exhaust. The sun was warm on her face even with her hood pulled forward. She followed the workers into the terminal. Several people stood by the entrance, a few holding signs. An old man with glasses and a mustache held one that read *Ditko/Kirby*, muttering to his neighbor that he was sure they were on *this* plane. On the other side of him, Maia saw a tall, rangy man with a neatly trimmed brown beard and a hockey mullet of a haircut holding a sign with her name written on it in black marker. Beside him stood a young woman who was more than a foot shorter than Maia and probably weighed a third as much. She was gorgeous to the point of distracting others. Elfin features, tawny hair, and flawless skin made her one of the most intimidating people Maia had ever seen. Both of them wore civilian attire with heavy zip-up black hoodies bearing the familiar blue oval logo of Just Cause on the breasts.

"Maia?" the man asked as she approached them.

"Yeah."

He extended his hand, looking her in the eye. He was nearly as tall as her. His accent suggested he was possibly Canadian. She knew JCAC was an international effort—the first team of its kind. "I'm Cale Davis, also known as Midnight Sun. I'm second in command of Just Cause Arctic Circle. This is Tanya Kamanev, Reindeer."

"Welcome to Deadhorse," the young woman said in a thick Russian accent. "You are Devilfish, yes? They did not tell me you were blue."

"Yeah." Maia felt even more self-conscious, like she was an impostor who had no right to be there.

"I like it," Tanya said firmly. "You look like . . . a sea elf."

"What's a sea elf?" Maia asked.

Tanya shrugged. "An elf who is blue, yes? Who looks like you. It is good thing to be."

Sea elf, Maia thought. That would have been such a good name if she'd thought of it. She wondered if it was too late to change from Devilfish. But no, elves were supposed to be tiny, delicate creatures, more like Tanya.

Maia was a whale.

"How was your flight?" Midnight Sun asked. *Cale*, Maia reminded herself. She didn't have to use their code names all the time, even though they were so much easier to remember.

"It was pretty long, yeah? I left first thing in the morning." Bright sunlight streamed through the terminal windows. "Feels like I've been traveling forever, but it's still daylight outside."

Cale checked his phone. "It's almost eleven PM, local time. Have you eaten? We've got plenty of food back at HQ, but we could get something here if you need."

"No thank you. They fed me on the plane. I'm fine. I'm just tired." She felt bone-weary, like she could have slept for a week.

"Plane food. Ugh." Cale smiled. "You change your mind, just let us know. We can do a lot better than that."

"Do you have another bag to collect?" Tanya asked.

"No, I've got everything here." Maia hefted her duffel bag. It held a small selection of clothes and toiletries, and two costumes. She didn't feel the cold and had no need to dress for it, even in the temperatures that would be prevalent at the height of Arctic winter. She'd been tested down to minus a hundred fifty degrees Fahrenheit, which was far colder than any natural temperature the Earth could throw at her. Instead of dressing for warmth, she preferred to dress for comfort. In her case, comfort included baggy, oversized hoodies into which she could disappear when she felt too obviously inhuman.

She followed Cale and Tanya out to a black SUV in the lot with the Just Cause logo on the doors. It wasn't sitting in a special section or sequestered; it was just parked in line with the other vehicles. It was a mundane thing, but it helped Maia to feel a little less alien. The lot wasn't paved like it would have been back in the Lower Forty-Eight. Instead it was made from crushed and compacted gravel. As she looked around, she saw that everything seemed to be sitting on a thick layer of gravel and asked about it, curious in spite of her travel exhaustion.

"It spreads out the weight of the buildings," Cale said. "Otherwise when the top layer thaws in the summer, you'd have buildings sinking into the mud all the time. We're just getting to the warm season now. Mud everywhere. Did you see all the lakes and ponds when you flew in?"

Maia nodded.

"When the top layer of earth thaws, water can't sink lower because of the permafrost, so it just kind of sits there when it can't drain into a river basin. That makes bogs and mud. Then it freezes all over again." Cale slapped at something on his arm. "In the meantime, we have mosquitoes. Big ones. They'll team up to carry you back to their nest so they can feed on you later."

"Awful," Tanya said. "Cover up if they like your taste."

"They don't like me. At least, they didn't back home. I don't think they can bite through my skin, yeah?"

Cale waved an insect away from his face. "Lucky for you."

"Is because of all the maple syrup you eat," Tanya said. "*Moskity* like sugar." She nudged Maia. "He imports it."

Cale slipped behind the wheel and started the engine. "Oh, Canada."

* * *

Like all the other buildings in Deadhorse, Just Cause Arctic Circle Headquarters had a temporary look about it. It consisted of some twenty-five repurposed shipping containers that had been welded together to form a single large building. A pair of large Quonset huts sat off to one side, which Cale said were vehicle storage. They were long, broad hemispherical buildings, like someone had cut off the top part of a cylinder and stuck doors on the flat part. He drove the SUV up to one of them and used a low-tech garage door opener to roll up the door.

The inside of the motor pool looked like every other garage Maia had seen, with a concrete floor, tanks for various fluids, and racks of tools. Besides the space for their current SUV, the garage contained a second SUV, a lifted full-size van with lumpy off-road tires, and a tracked machine she thought was called a snowcat. Removable snowplow attachments lay against one wall. All the vehicles were plugged into reinforced cords, presumably to keep their engines warm.

"You plug them in even in the summer?" Maia asked as she watched Cale connect their SUV to the power cord.

"You never know when a cold snap will hit, and it's a good habit. You'll learn pretty quickly about following habits up here. They save lives."

"Do you have a plane? Or a boat?" Maia knew mobility was key for dispatching superhero teams quickly in emergencies. Other Just Cause teams had top-of-the-line VTOL jets for rapid deployment, but JCAC was new, and a combat-level aircraft was probably outside of the team's needs.

"We have a Jayhawk helicopter in the next hut over. It's the same model the Coast Guard uses. We named it the *Clara*, after Clara Bow. She was a silent film actress."

Maia nodded. Whomever had decided upon the naming conventions for Just Cause team aircraft was a fan of early film and World War II-style pinup art.

"Come with me," Tanya said. "We will get you settled into your room and meet the others."

"All right." Maia followed Tanya and Cale through a tunnel from the motor pool to the main building. It had thick foam insulation sprayed upon the walls and ceiling, making it feel like they were walking through a natural cave instead of man-made construction. Some humorist had scrawled *Welcome to the Frozen Wasteland* in permanent marker along one wall. Below that, in different handwriting, someone had added *If you lived here, you would be home by now.*

"It still gets cold in here," Cale said, noticing Maia's interest in the material. "I know your file says you don't feel the cold, and that's good—we've got a couple others like you here—but some of us are a little more delicate."

"I hate the cold," Tanya added.

"Where are you from?" Maia asked.

"Siberia."

"Wow, really? Isn't it cold there?"

"Yes. I hate it. I want to live on Mediterranean coast instead."

"Not much snow to run on there," Cale said.

"I will retire and look at cute cabana boys all day." Tanya smiled.

Cale opened the door into the main headquarters building. "We're a true international team. With so much shipping in the Arctic and eight different nations bordering the territory, the Powers That Be felt it would be a good concession to international cooperation to bring in some heroes from around the region. I'm Canadian, from Winnipeg."

"And his hockey team still sucks," said a man in the lounge-type room they entered. He was short and stout, with dark hair and a goatee. He had a bowl of popcorn and was watching Japanese baseball on a big-screen television.

Cale snorted in amusement, clearly used to conversation of that sort. "Maia, this is Harry Daughtry, also known as Igloo, and card-carrying fan of the Minnesota Wild, who missed the playoffs yet again."

Harry brushed popcorn crumbs off his hands and waved at Maia. "I'd shake hands, but I'm all buttery. I'm a snow and ice shaper. I can't create it out of thin air like Snowball can, but I do all right for the most part."

"Devilfish, but you can call me Maia," Maia said. She didn't know anything about hockey and didn't know what else to say.

"Nice to meet you. Welcome to the Great White North."

"That's Canada, you dingleberry," Cale said.

"Don't worry about upsetting him," Harry said in a mock aside. "He's Canadian. He'll eventually apologize."

"Sorry, what?" Cale grinned.

Harry smiled back at him. "Maia, you want some popcorn? Might want to grab a bowl before Burleigh gets back from the can and inhales the rest of it."

"No, thank you."

Tanya rolled her eyes. "Come, Maia. You have the room next to mine."

"Bring her back here in ten. I'll rustle up the rest of the team so we can make introductions," Cale said.

Harry set down his bowl. "Guess I'll make more popcorn, then."

Maia followed Tanya out of the lounge. The interior of the building was much more comfortable than it appeared from outside. The walls were well-insulated, and Tanya told her the floor was heated for the winter months. Maia would have thought something like that might be wasteful, but then she guessed oil was probably a cheap and plentiful resource in the area, given it was the foundation of all local industry.

"The whole facility is on stilts," Tanya said. "To keep us from melting into ground in summer."

That was a problem Maia would never have considered. She knew she had a lot to learn about life in the Arctic.

The residences wing of JCAC headquarters gave each hero a container room of their own. They were carpeted and included basic furnishings as well as a private bathroom suite. It looked like a bare hotel room with a double bed, cabinet, dresser, desk with a computer workstation, and a chair. "Seems . . . comfortable." Maia set her bag down on the bed. It was bigger than her dorm room had been but somehow seemed smaller because there was no window.

"Is terrible, yes. You should paint. Put up posters. Get a plant. Good *feng shui*." Tanya chuckled.

"What's that?"

"It means the good environment of a room. What is word? Harmony." Tanya went across the hall to open the door to her own room. "See, this is my room. Good *feng shui*."

Maia peeked into her neighbor's room. As Tanya had suggested, her walls were heavily decorated with posters from movies. Many of them had Cyrillic lettering, suggesting they'd come from her home instead of from American sources. She had pinned a couple colorful shawls into the upper corners of the room, softening the corners and giving it more of a cozy tent-like feel. A thick burgundy and blue afghan was folded at the foot of the bed, ready for warmth deployment at a moment's notice. A bright sunlamp spread its brilliance over a half dozen green leafy plants in pots sitting atop her workstation. Tanya zipped across the room, far faster than a normal human could move, and retrieved a couple pieces of dirty laundry to deposit in the hamper in the corner.

"This is nice," Maia said. "Where did you get all this stuff?"

"I bring some from Russia, buy some online. No two-day shipping here though." Tanya grinned. "You must be patient."

"I don't really have anything to decorate my room."

"I will help you fix that. What do you like best?"

Maia shrugged. "I don't know. Music, I guess. Classic rock, yeah?"

Tanya made a face. "That is boy music."

Maia felt her face grow hot. "Well, I like it."

Tanya shrugged. "Is good if you want to meet boys, I guess. There are many boys here in Alaska." She snickered. "Not many worth meeting though."

"I'm not here to meet boys, yeah?"

"Good. You will not waste your time that way. Instead, we will find you some posters. Good posters, to make your walls pretty." Tanya spotted something else potentially incriminating and blurred into motion as she picked it up and put it in her bathroom. "I apologize. I am messy."

"It's okay. You do you."

Tanya tilted her head sideways as she considered Maia's words. "I do not know that phrase."

"It means . . . I guess it means you do whatever pleases you, yeah?"

Tanya laughed. "You do you. Yes, you do you and I do me and we do us. Good times."

Maia laughed too. Without even knowing exactly how she'd managed it, it appeared she'd made a new friend.

Chapter Three

From Maia's playlist: "I Am the Walrus" - <u>The Beatles</u>

Just Cause Arctic Circle only had six members in total before Maia's arrival, and they were led by the smallest woman Maia had ever seen. Snowball was an honest-to-God little person. She didn't like the word *midget* but didn't get as angry about it as some of her fellows in the community, she said. She dropped the tidbit of trivia that the incidence of parahuman powers in little people was about ten times that of regular humans, and she said that was the Universe's way of balancing things out. Sara Gunnarsson was as unapologetic and crass as she was short. She said she was trying to work on her swearing, but when she was surrounded by oil riggers and roughnecks, sometimes it got pretty fucking difficult to control her fucking mouth. She'd thought about implementing a swear jar, she said, but didn't carry enough cash, to which Harry retorted he wasn't sure there *was* enough cash.

As Harry had described, Sara was an ice *creator.* Sheets of it, constructions—she could even transport herself and others on it by generating a constantly moving slide in a technique she called *ice surfing.* She could form it out of thin air, whether or not there was any moisture in the air to work with—although she could create significantly more ice when it was humid. "So naturally, they sent me up here to the Arctic desert," she said with a laugh. "I probably pissed off too many of the wrong people. I'm good at that." JCAC was her first command and her fourth Just Cause team. She'd also been part of Denver, New York, and Chicago. "Basically, I'm going to progressively worse environments. I fully expect my next assignment will be on the Moon."

Maia already knew Cale's superhero name of Midnight Sun and that he was Canadian. She learned he could also fly and true to his name, generated his own light. She hadn't noticed it in the airport or when he'd brought her to headquarters, but he did have a faint glow about him in the lounge, and he brightened it for a moment so she could see it more clearly. "I'm not really as bright as the sun," he admitted. "But I make a pretty good searchlight. When I concentrate, I can focus my light a little more in a single direction." Despite being able to generate energy, it wasn't useful for anything except illumination. His power didn't lend itself to offensive use. "Maybe if I had a magnifying glass and a target that wasn't trying to kill me, I could burn a tiny hole in it given enough time."

Harry showed Maia how, as Igloo, he could reshape the ball of ice Sara made for him. He recast it first from a sphere into a cube, and then into a representation of an airplane. The ice sang as he shaped it, the way icy rivers and lakes did when temperatures changed. "Long as there's a source, I can make pretty much anything I can visualize out of ice," he said.

"You should try to visualize an effective power play unit for the Wild," Cale said. "Sorry, don't mean to interrupt."

"At least we don't have a revolving door of goaltenders," Harry retorted.

Sara slapped an impatient fist onto the table beside her. "Boys, please, could we go through one night without a goddamn hockey reference? Yes, you're fans. We *all* know you're fans. Just compare the size of your sticks on your own time, not mine."

Maia smiled. She didn't mind the banter. She wasn't any good at it herself, but it was fun to listen to. It reminded her of being back at the Academy among her classmates.

Tanya turned to her. "As you know, I am Russian, and I have nothing to do with your elections. That is little joke I like to tell."

"Very little," said a brawny dark-skinned man lounging in a chair that could barely contain him. He hadn't yet introduced himself.

"Keep your size-ist jokes to yourself, Burleigh," Sara said in a tone that suggested she was sorry she hadn't made it first.

"I am also a speedster, but you of course already know this. I can run on snow like Legolas the Elf."

"Who?" Maia asked.

"He goes to find the sun. We will watch it, you and I." Tanya smiled. "He is very nice to look at."

"Uh, okay." Maia felt like she'd missed something, but didn't know what. At least she didn't think Tanya was making fun of her.

"Burleigh Carnes," said the big man from the recliner. He had black sideburns, mustache, and beard, and his hair was all cut the same length, like he went over it with a trimmer daily. A scar ran up his forehead from just above his left eye to travel halfway across his scalp. The scar wasn't broad or disgusting, but it stood out in the gentle lighting of the lounge. The hair along the edges of the scar was white, making it even more noticeable against his brown skin. "Snowcat. I'm a typical brick, because every team needs one. I'm the world's last black lumberjack."

"Really?" Maia hated how gullible she sounded as soon as she said it.

"Naw, but I do have an axe. Canadian steel foundry made it for me. Thing's nearly indestructible."

"It's certainly unharmed by the vicious local trees," Harry said.

Cale looked apologetic. "There aren't any trees this far north. They can't grow in this climate."

"Oh." Maia was beginning to feel out of her depth again. She wished she could go take a dip in the ocean. Clear her head. Get away from the attention and the exhausting social interaction.

"I'm Michelle Seiko," said the last member Maia hadn't yet met but seemed familiar somehow. "I go by Simulcast." Then Maia remembered. Simulcast had graduated the same year Maia started at the Academy, making her two years older. Her hair was dyed greenish blue and hung around her face in an unkempt mop. She had an exotic appearance that came from a mixed Japanese-Mexican ancestry, courtesy of the melting pot that was San Francisco. "I can hear and transmit radio signals. And I hate it here."

Grumbling from around the room suggested this was not news to any of the rest of the team.

"I'm a warm-weather girl. I'm only here because I pissed off the wrong people."

Sara cleared her throat. "You're here because your powers make you invaluable to this team. We've had this discussion before. When someone else comes up with your abilities—*if* that ever happens—we will rotate you out to a warm-weather team. In all honesty, there isn't a Just Cause team anywhere that wouldn't need you with your abilities. I'm happy you're here."

"I'm not!" Michelle said. "There's a hurricane coming!"

Sara muttered something abrupt and probably offensive under her breath.

Michelle's statement made the entire room go silent. The heroes of Just Cause Arctic Circle looked at each other in confusion.

"How can there be a hurricane here?" Maia asked. "Doesn't there have to be warm water?"

"They happen in the winter," Tanya said. "Very scary then. Strong and powerful, but short-lived."

"It's not unheard of for them to roll through in the summer. Lots of rain and sleet, and wind that'll knock you over," Harry said. "It's really early in the season for one, though."

Maia, who had never been close enough to a coast to deal with hurricane weather, stayed quiet. She'd seen news reports about the hurricanes that hit the Gulf States and along the East Coast in the past year, but she'd been in Denver, where the worst thing they had was hail and an occasional tornado. Before that she'd lived in northeastern California where they didn't see much of anything except rain during the winters. She'd have been much more concerned if there had been a wildfire coming, but there weren't any trees to burn.

"Weather stations in the Archipelago have been tracking the depression for the past six hours. It's been steadily increasing in strength. We're looking at a full-scale Arctic cyclone here in the next two days." Michelle tapped the side of her head, probably listening to a broadcast with her powers.

"And you were going to tell us when?" Sara glowered at her teammate.

"Told you now, didn't I?"

Maia raised her hand.

"This isn't school, Maia," Cale said, not unkindly. "You don't have to be called on to speak. What's on your mind?"

"I was just, uh, wondering what we have to do in a hurricane."

Michelle shrugged. "Lots of searching and rescuing, probably. Terrible internet connectivity, so Netflix is going to suck."

Sara sighed, then looked at Maia. "Well, this is why we're here, everyone. Welcome to Just Cause, Devilfish. Looks like you showed up just in time."

* * *

Sara ordered Maia to be ready for duty by seven o'clock the next morning. Maia gratefully fell asleep in her unadorned bedroom and when her alarm woke her, she had slept so hard she hadn't moved a muscle. For once, she was grateful to be bald. If she'd had to take the time to fix her hair, she might have been late for her first day.

Food was plentiful and of good quality in the cafeteria. Burleigh was eating his way through a mountain of scrambled eggs and hash browns with a separate plate of sausages and bacon. "Have a seat, Devilfish," he said after swallowing a mouthful. "Plenty to go around. You'll burn through it up here. Always a lot of work to be done."

"It's Maia," she said, and made herself a plate. The eggs were probably reconstituted and the potatoes from a bag, but everything was prepared well. The sausage had an unusual but not unpleasant flavor profile. "These are good."

"They're caribou," Burleigh said. "Protein-dense. Good for us over-muscled types." He flexed one arm and his muscles creaked against the insulated undershirt he wore. "You're super-strong, aren't you?"

Maia nodded. "Strong, tough, and immune to cold temperatures."

"And you swim? Kinda figured it with your name."

"Yeah."

"That's good." He lowered his voice, glancing around to make sure none of the other heroes were within earshot. "I can't swim."

"Is that a secret?"

He nodded. "I can't go around tellin' people that. I'd be a walkin' stereotype. A black man who can't swim? I might as well eat watermelon and fried chicken for every meal." He paused. "Actually, that doesn't sound too bad."

"I like watermelon and fried chicken too," Maia said. "Your secret is safe with me, yeah." She took a bite of food. "What will we be doing today and tomorrow?"

"Whatever's needed," Burleigh said. "The oil workers know how much time they need to seal everything up in advance of the storm. We won't help with that unless there's an emergency. The riggers will evacuate from the platforms, and we'll keep an eye on that in case someone needs help. For the most part, we'll just be standing around on call."

Despite Burleigh's promise of a quiet couple of days, Maia found that the team members were quite busy. Michelle stayed in the Command Center, coordinating communications between the various rig crews and directing shipping to safer areas. Unlike in the Caribbean, sea ice made fleeing to safer waters more difficult and dangerous, and like an air traffic controller, she had to keep the cruise ships, cargo vessels, and tankers from getting too close to each other. She also monitored the approaching storm and gave out regular updates as to wind speed and estimated time of landfall. The approaching storm had been named Polar Cyclone Advent, which was a surprisingly Christmas-y name for a summertime storm. Maia asked her about it and Michelle said that they traditionally used holiday-themed names for Arctic storms.

Cale's powers weren't especially useful during the 24-hour daylight of the Arctic summer, so he stayed in the Command Center as well, keeping in constant contact with Canadian authorities to help with coordination on their end. Tanya acted as a gopher for work crews, bringing them emergency tools or supplies as required while they worked to seal off the wells and buildings ahead of the approaching storm. Instead of her costume, she wore lightweight wind- and water-resistant clothing, like what windsurfers wore, colored a bright yellow and orange so she would be clearly visible to workers and vehicle operators. "Why not wear your costume?" Maia asked her.

"It has antlers. Is stupid. I only wear it when officially dispatched," Tanya said.

"Why not change it to something you don't hate, yeah?"

"It is assigned uniform. My government requires it of me. At least I do not also have to wear clown nose."

"Clown nose? Oh! Like Rudolph the Red-nosed Reindeer." Maia laughed.

Sara and Harry worked together to shore up buildings, she by creating massive ice blocks and he by shaping them into windbreaks and levees. They would erode under the onslaught of the storm, but would deflect the worst of the energy away from the buildings of Deadhorse and the oilfields to the north. They rolled around town in one of the Just Cause SUVs like a couple of gangsters, blasting music as they worked.

Maia worked alongside Burleigh to help seal off the wells. She asked Burleigh if she should wear her costume for it, but he said no, and got her a set of orange coveralls with a matching hard hat and uncomfortable steel-toed boots. They were required by OSHA, he said, and they had to abide by those requirements while working on the rigs. The two of them were as effective as a crane and could wrestle large steel plates into place so the crews could weld them together. It was hard, repetitive work and even though Maia was graced with super-strength and endurance to match, at the end of a shift, her muscles ached like they never had during her hardest training sessions at the Academy. She felt like the knots in her back might never untangle themselves.

Burleigh patted her shoulder. "Good work today, kid. We may just get through this yet. By this time tomorrow, everythin' ought to be sealed up and ready to ride out the storm."

Maia smiled. She'd received several compliments on her work from riggers, most of whom didn't seem to have any problem with her odd physical appearance. She'd seen one man who had so many tattoos that his skin was nearly the same shade as hers. She wanted to go look at all the pictures and words decorating his flesh but was too shy to approach him. They were there to work, and living in the Arctic for weeks at a time meant they were psychologically stable enough to accept the weird with equanimity. A couple men had looked sidelong at her, but nobody said anything offensive to the girl wrestling twelve-hundred-pound sheets of steel like they were plywood. She didn't feel like part of the team yet, but at least she didn't feel like the outsider she'd been growing up back in California. Burleigh made a special effort to help her feel included, always making sure she had enough to eat at meals and always there with water or coffee when needed. He was like a watchful big brother. When she asked him about it, he said he had seven younger siblings and had grown up with his head on a swivel, always watching out for the young'uns.

Still, even for a brick like herself, it was hard work and she nodded off in the middle of her dinner. Burleigh shook her awake and asked if she wanted to finish her plate. She remembered saying yes but then nodded off again. She had a faint memory of Burleigh and Tanya helping her to her room and then she passed out into blissful, exhausted sleep.

Chapter Four

From Maia's playlist: "The Wind Cries Mary"
- The Jimi Hendrix Experience

By the next day, everyone was just calling it Hurricane Advent, because *Polar Cyclone* didn't feel like it carried enough weight. A cyclone was the goofy looking cottony thing from *The Wizard of Oz* movie. A hurricane was nature's greatest force of destruction, and as it barreled down toward Prudhoe Bay, Maia felt like she was standing at ground zero for a nuclear bomb test. With no night to hide behind, the clouds spread across the horizon as they drew closer and closer. Wind speeds in the storm increased from eighty to a hundred miles per hour over the first half of the day. In the past two hours, with the comparatively warm Arctic Ocean feeding the hungry engine driving the storm, wind speeds had accelerated to a blistering hundred and forty miles per hour. They circled around what meteorologists called a well-formed eyewall. That made it the equivalent of a Category Four storm, and even Maia understood that was serious.

"What's it going to be like?" she asked Burleigh as the two of them sat at the edge of a rig they'd just finished sealing and watched the distant clouds. They were still far enough away not to look particularly threatening, although there was a heavy darkness beneath them that made Maia uneasy. The prevailing Arctic wind was cold, but maybe not as cold as it might have been. Patches of snow and ice along the edges of some of the buildings steadily shrank as the wind ate away at them, leaving behind puddles and shallow ponds.

"Windy, probably," Burleigh said. "Like a good old-fashioned nor'easter back home."

Maia watched as a family of Arctic foxes ran across the gravel—three kittens and a pair of adults, one of whom was carrying an unfortunate rabbit—and disappeared beneath a building. She'd seen them before, sunning themselves on cement pads. They were comfortable enough around humans that they didn't run unless approached. She hoped they would weather the storm okay. They were brown and gray for the summer and Harry said they wouldn't turn white until the end of the warm season.

"I've never been in a nor'easter. We barely even got snow where I grew up. Will there be rain? Snow?"

Burleigh shrugged. "Honestly, I don't know. I've only seen winter storms, and they're scary as hell. Whiteout so bad you can't see a buildin' that's ten feet away from you."

Maia's eyes widened. "What do you do then?"

"We don't go outside. Nobody does. They shut everything down, just like they're doin' now. Stay indoors, stay safe, play games and wait it out."

"Maybe some of the workers know what to expect, yeah?"

"I don't think anybody really knows what to expect anymore. Michelle was sayin' there didn't used to be bad storms like this in the summer, but it's happenin' more often."

Maia had read a lot about climate change when she'd finally been allowed to start studying real science. She couldn't believe how bad humans were messing up the planet. She wondered if there were any weather-controlling superheroes who could make a difference. They'd have to be able to work on a global scale, and from what she'd learned at the Hero Academy, that kind of power level simply didn't exist within the spectrum of parahuman powers. "That's why they sent us up here, yeah? To watch out for all the shipping and oil workers and things."

"No doubt. Riggers say every year there are more people up here, more ships passin' through the straits. Accidents are bound to happen. They'll need folks like us to help them." Burleigh got to his feet and tapped his radio. "Snowcat and Devilfish checkin' in. You need us anywhere else or are we about done with the prep work?"

"You two better get back here on the double," Michelle said. "There's trouble brewing."

Burleigh glanced at the gathering clouds and snorted. "Yeah, we're lookin' at it. Wall to wall clouds."

"Not that kind of trouble. We just picked up a distress call."

Burleigh frowned. "That's not good." He held a hand out to Maia to help her to her feet. "Looks like it's time to go do some *real* work for some folks that need our help."

* * *

The Command Center was a flurry of activity. All six civilian employees who worked rotating shifts in the center had been called in, and they sat at their terminals checking weather reports, reviewing shipping lanes, and speaking into their headsets. A couple of them looked like they'd been called in the middle of their sleep periods, and were alternately yawning or sipping from mugs of coffee. Maia and Burleigh got back to headquarters just after Tanya, while Sara and Harry ice-surfed their way back in from the oilfield.

Cale and Michelle were marking lines on a map on the big screen along with a pair of staffers. They looked super busy so Maia sidled up beside Tanya, who stood off to one side so she wouldn't be in the way. "What's going on?"

"There is a ship out there somewhere. Michelle said they reported a fire on board and are adrift. Their radio is also damaged and they cannot receive messages, only send," the Russian said. "Advent is close. They are in great danger." She looked up at Maia. "We should prepare to depart."

"There's a lot of ocean out there, and the storm isn't going to hit all of it. Do we know for sure they're actually in the storm's path?" Cale asked Michelle as one of the staffers moved lines on the map.

Michelle shrugged. "I only got the one transmission, and it was pretty garbled. I can't be sure of the location except they're somewhere in this area." She pointed to a long, narrow triangle that originated at the dot representing JCAC headquarters. "That's the direction the transmission came from."

"No emergency beacon?"

"Nothing, no. Maybe they can fix it." A staffer connected several lines and filled in an area of the map showing Advent's likeliest path. If the stranded ship indeed lay within Michelle's area, it wasn't looking good for them.

Sara and Harry hurried into the Command Center. "It doesn't matter where they are in relation to the storm," Cale said. "Being that close to it, they might as well be staring down the barrel of a gun. We've got to go get them."

"Fill me in," Sara said immediately. Cale told her what little information they had. "No question, we've got to get them. The storm track goes right across that path. If they're not already getting beaten to shit by the waves, they're going to be in a couple of hours. It's going to be ugly by the time we get there. Everyone, gear up for an ocean rescue." Michelle started to protest and Sara shut her down immediately. "You too, Seiko. We need you to track any signals we get once we're in the air."

"Should I wear my costume?" Maia asked Tanya.

"It is for swimming, yes?"

"Yeah."

"Then I think so."

Although JCAC had locker rooms for costumes, Maia hadn't yet moved hers there, so she went back to her quarters to dress. Her costume was subtle and streamlined for ease of movement in the water. For all intents and purposes it was a scuba-diving suit made from the kevlar-weave fabric preferred by the Just Cause costuming division. Although ocean water didn't harm Maia, the costume was sheathed in a waterproof, friction-reducing seal that allowed her to swim faster than if she didn't wear it at all. It was modeled after whale coloring—dark gray on the back and pale gray on the front. A blue Just Cause oval logo was printed on each shoulder. Small, rigid fin-like extensions emerged from the outsides of her hips, shoulder blades, and her shins to help reduce cavitation and to give her better directional control when she swam at speed.

She had special gloves with webbing between the fingers and fins on the forearms, and soft boots with fin extensions on the ankles as well. Although she often swam with a standard freestyle stroke, when she really needed speed, she switched to an underwater butterfly, kicking her legs up and down like she was a mermaid or a porpoise. Her best speed out of costume was just under thirty miles per hour, using nothing but her brute strength to haul herself through the water. When she wore the highly engineered outfit, she could double that speed. Racing through the water as fast as a speedboat was as exhilarating an experience as she'd ever encountered in her life, and she looked forward to every opportunity to do so.

She strapped the swimming cap over her head. It had a built-in air supply that could provide her with one additional lungful of compressed air. That might not seem like much, but with her ability to hold her breath for almost half an hour, it doubled her time to stay below without surfacing. The incorporated visor corrected for water-based distortion, allowing her to see nearly as well underwater as she could above it. Where many hero costumes incorporated a utility belt or hip pouches for gear, her pouch rode beneath her breasts. It was designed to give her a more streamlined shape but made her look even fatter. She hated that portion of the costume but understood the reasoning behind it. She carried in it a selection of waterproof Just Cause-approved gear. A standard-issue emergency beacon was incorporated into the costume on top of her thigh where it wouldn't be likely to catch on anything.

Still feeling a little modest around people she didn't yet know well, she slipped a standard-issue Just Cause windbreaker over the ensemble and regarded herself in her mirror. She still thought her costume looked more strange than heroic, but she'd found an identity in it, and it helped with her general feelings of inadequacy. "You're a superhero," she said. "Don't be afraid to act like one."

She left her room and made her way back through the tunnel toward the motor pool and hangar. She could hear the sound of a helicopter warming up and her heart started to race. She'd never been on a helicopter before and didn't know what to expect. Wind and dust blew into her face as she exited the tunnel into the hangar. The helicopter had already been wheeled out onto the pad in front of the big door and the side door was open. Tanya waved at her from within, indicating she should hurry over. Maia ran across the pad to climb in before she gave herself a chance to think twice.

Tanya handed her a pair of headphones with a microphone in front. She wore a set herself, and they looked almost comically oversized on the petite Russian girl.

"I have not seen your costume before," Tanya said, her voice crackling through the headphones louder than the muffled sound of the rotors overhead. "I like it. You look like a whale."

"Thanks." Maia lowered her head in shame even though she knew Tanya hadn't meant to cause offense.

"I did not mean to insult." Tanya touched her hand. "You look strong, and fearless, like you belong in the ocean."

"I know what you meant, yeah." Maia made herself smile. "They used to call gray whales *devilfish* because of how they fought."

"How do you fight?"

"Badly." Maia laughed. "I'm terrible at combat. Barely passed my class at the Academy, yeah?"

"I received military training in Moscow," Tanya said. "Although we do not have a formalized school for parahumans in Russia. Our training is more individualized and tailored for our needs. It is efficient but perhaps not as enjoyable as yours."

"Are you good at fighting?"

"I am adequate. Mostly I am best at staying around edges to take shots of opportunity. I cannot take a punch as well as some." Tanya smiled. Tanya's own costume was a tight-fitting dun-colored suit with reinforced panels at her joints and over her chest. She wore a headband with small antlers on it. Maia raised an eyebrow as she looked at them. She'd heard Tanya say her costume had antlers before, but she hadn't really considered what that meant. Tanya's cheeks colored. "I know they look stupid, but I am under obligation to wear them. I am a representative of Russia and must maintain my state-approved image."

She said *state-approved image* with such sarcasm that Maia was a little surprised a commissar didn't pop up to berate her for failing to appropriately glorify her homeland. "They're not terrible."

Tanya sniffed. "I lose them at every opportunity. I hope eventually replacing them becomes too expensive."

The others boarded the helicopter. Their costumes seemed more like colorful insulated coveralls than the spandex-and-kevlar suits preferred by heroes of lower latitudes. Each was unique in its way, perhaps reminiscent of what they might have worn outside the Arctic. Sara's coveralls were ice blue and trimmed with white fur at the collar, wrists, and ankles, almost making her look like a miniature snow bunny. She had a white knit hat with straps holding it under her chin like a helmet. She also wore a backpack and her pockets bulged with gear.

Burleigh dressed like a cliché lumberjack, all the way down to the checkered shirt, leather work gloves, and the cap with earmuffs. He had a large axe made entirely of gray metal hanging from a strap over one shoulder. He smiled cheerfully as he set the headphones over his ears. His sleeves were rolled up like he was ready to get busy chopping down trees.

Cale's sky blue bodysuit darkened to black at his hands and feet. He had a black cowl that covered his entire face, leaving traditional white slits for his eyes. A blue hood went over his cowled head, accompanied by a short blue cape that ended at his waist. His suit incorporated a stylized sun insignia. He looked the most like a superhero out of any of them, which meant his costume was old-fashioned compared to the modern, highly engineered and test-marketed looks of contemporary heroes.

Harry and Michelle were the last to board the 'copter. Harry wore an orange parka with a furred hood and goggles, looking like a stereotypical Arctic explorer. Michelle dressed in a full red snowsuit with a scarf and stocking cap and an expression of pure disgust.

"Are we all comfy?" Sara asked as she tightened straps on the seat custom-designed to hold someone of her stature.

"Good to go, boss," Cale said.

"Mikhail, get this bird in the air," Sara said into her microphone. "Sooner we find this boat, the sooner we can all go home and button up the base until the storm blows over."

The pilot, whose Russian accent was much thicker than Tanya's, said, "*Da*, here ve go, liddies and gents."

The *Clara*'s engine rose to a shriek and the helicopter lurched into the sky, heading northeast into the storm.

Chapter Five

From Maia's playlist: "Ship of Fools" - <u>Grateful Dead</u>

Over the course of the next hour, Maia learned a bunch of things. Some were obvious: helicopters were super loud, even with the headphones on to make conversation with her teammates possible. She was getting a headache and wished she could just dive into the ocean to get away from the noise. Other things she was sorry to learn, such as how Tanya, who had seemed so confident and self-assured since they'd first met, got horribly airsick. The Russian speedster spent most of the flight with her head down, occasionally retching into a bag. The others politely ignored her discomfort. Turbulence on an airplane was nothing compared to turbulence on a helicopter. They all got bounced around as winds and rain battered against it. Mikhail, the pilot, warned them it was going to affect their speed and their range, and not in a good way.

"Forty-five knots, with gusts up to sixty," he said. "Cut safe range to less than five hundred kilometers."

"Understood, Mikhail," Sara said. "We'll just have to find them before we run out of gas."

"Temperature dropping. Rain vill become sleet soon. Vill make flying very dangerous."

"Imagine what it must be like for the crew of the *Atlanta Nights*," Cale said. "Stranded with a dead engine and no power and wondering if anyone will come for them before Advent catches up to them."

"I did not say I vould not get you there." Mikhail sounded offended. "I said it vould be dangerous."

"Danger is my middle name," Burleigh said.

"Really?" Harry asked. "Mine's Callahan, and yes, I know. My dad loved those movies."

"What movies?" Maia asked.

"*Dirty Harry*. They're about a tough-as-nails cop who bucks the system to get justice with a hand cannon."

"Boy movies," Tanya said, burped, and bent forward again to address her airsick bag.

"What kind of name is *Atlanta Nights* for a tramp freighter? It sounds like a fucking joke," Sara said.

"I don't know," Michelle said. "It's all I got before their transmitter shit the bed. I keep listening but nobody's making any noise out there. All the smart fishes are already swimming away."

"Is the storm interfering with your powers?" Maia asked.

"Every time lightning flashes, it's like someone is poking my face with a stick, so yeah." Michelle grimaced. "There's a lot of lightning."

The *Clara* flew onward into the wind. The storm spread out before and above them, a wall of dark clouds lit from within by lightning and bright white at the top where the sun still shone upon them.

"Vind speed increasing to fifty-five knots," Mikhail warned as he fought with the control lever. "I can give you twenty-five more minutes and then ve must turn about."

"We're not leaving anybody out here," Sara said. "We'll find a way."

"Not unless you find more fuel. Math is math," Mikhail said. "Vait . . . ping on radar."

Sara undid her straps. "I'm coming up there to help you look."

"Be careful. Vind is very unpredictable." As if to illustrate Mikhail's warning, a gust shook the *Clara* like a dog shaking a stuffed toy, and Tanya bowed her head into her bag once more. Rain battered against the canopy like someone throwing gravel at it. The cabin temperature cooled quickly and condensation formed on the inside of the windows. Burleigh wiped one next to him with his sleeve and peered into the storm, trying to see anything below the swirling clouds and driving rain.

"There!" Sara called. "Two o'clock from our current heading."

"*Da*, I see." The 'copter dipped, shedding altitude as it approached a small blue and white freighter with a cabin aft and a half dozen containers lashed atop the deck. Maia could see it through the rain-lashed window. She thought of it as small, but she had next to no experience with boats and wouldn't know what to compare it to.

"Devilfish? Hey, Earth to Maia."

Maia startled and looked around, feeling her face flush with embarrassment. The whole team was looking at her and Sara, who had just called to her, frowned with impatience. She might have crossed her arms in disapproval if she didn't need them to stay braced in the cockpit door.

"I'm sorry," Maia mumbled.

"I know it's kind of daunting, this being your first call-out," Sara said. "But it's why we're here. How confident a swimmer are you? Can you swim in this sea? Can you get to the surface if you need us to pick you out of the water? Don't lie and tell me you can do it if you can't. I don't need a dead hero today. Or any day."

Maia wiped her own window and looked down at the water. The sea was choppy, with the boat below swaying to and fro as wind-driven swells battered against it. "I can handle it, yeah." She knew she could; there was nothing to be gained by lying about her powers in an emergency. If she could do something, she needed to say so, and if she couldn't . . . well, she needed to be honest about that too. Far more lives than her own were at stake.

"I don't like that we haven't seen so much as a flare," Cale said. "Surely they can hear us by now."

"Still nothing on the radio," Michelle said. "That ship is dead in the water."

"All right," Sara said. "I don't like the way it's shifting back and forth. Maia, you hit ocean and board it from water level. Cale, fly down to it. I will try to build up some ice pontoons to keep it stable, but nothing is going to help much in this weather. Bring anyone who's alive back up to the deck and we'll bring them up via the sling. Let's move, people. This fucking storm is only going to get worse."

Burleigh opened the side door and freezing wind blasted into the cabin, making everyone else draw their coats and hoods tighter around them. Cale flew out into the storm, igniting his primary power as he did so. He shone like a star amid the clouds, brilliant and hot enough to make steam rise off him. He descended toward the listing *Atlanta Nights*' deck.

"Maia, go," Sara said.

Maia threw off her jacket and stepped up to the edge of the cabin. The landing skid was right below her and she didn't want to get hung up upon it. The rotors overhead made her feel like she was standing beneath a blender. Without giving herself too much time to think about how she was *diving into the Arctic Ocean during a hurricane*, she jumped clear of the 'copter.

The impact into the water didn't hurt, even though she'd fallen a dozen meters. She could have belly flopped the landing and it wouldn't have hurt, either. The icy cold didn't bother her, but the sudden temperature change still shocked her as she knifed into it, hands over her head like a wedge. The waves closed over her. Her ears filled with the muted, echoing sounds of the deep and she saw the strange patterns of diffuse light from the choppy seas overhead. She watched them swirl through her goggles for a moment, then kicked her feet and pushed back to the surface.

She broke the plane between sea and sky and let the swirling waves carry her for a moment while she got her bearings. Small pieces of sea ice floated on the surface, surrounded by clumps of slush. The helicopter hovered a dozen yards above her. Mikhail struggled to keep it level and steady as the wind howled around it. The *Atlanta Nights* listed maybe fifty feet off to her left. *Port*, she told herself. At sea, *left* was *port*. She took a deep breath, compressing air into her lungs with a single massive inhalation, and dove back under the surface.

In the ocean, she felt free and relaxed for the first time since she'd arrived in Deadhorse. She'd been so uptight for so long, feeling the pressure of the expectations laid upon her as a graduate of the Hero Academy. She might not have felt much like a superhero, but the Parahuman Resources Administration wouldn't have assigned her to JCAC if they hadn't felt she was up to snuff. Still, the stress of needing to impress the others of the team seemed far away. It was a problem for the surface world, not one for Maia's peace beneath the waves. Even the storm raging overhead felt distant, insulated from her by twenty feet of water.

She spotted *Atlanta Nights'* keel and swam to it. It looked like it had seen better days. A few barnacles clung to nooks on the underside, and there was one good-sized dent where it must have run aground on a reef, sandbar, or ice floe. She surfaced beside the hull and a spotlight shone upon her from above as Cale spotted her and directed his light in her direction. She waved at him. He split his light into two beams, one pointing at her and the other thirty feet to her right where ladder rungs were bolted to the hull. She swam to them and climbed up the side of the lurching craft.

Atlanta Nights had looked tiny from the helicopter window, and it wasn't a large ship compared to the massive supertankers that plied the world's oceans, but it seemed plenty large to Maia. It was some two hundred fifty feet long and thirty wide. The crew probably stayed in the cabins aft while cargo containers filled the main deck and probably one or two lower decks as well.

Cale landed next to Maia, shielding his eyes from the blowing rain. "This ship has no business being here," he shouted to be heard over the roar of the wind and the nearby helicopter. "This is a coastal vessel."

"I guess they're really lost, yeah?" Maia said.

Cale had a radio clipped to his shoulder like a police officer and he spoke into it. "We're here and beginning our search. Mikhail, what's our fuel situation, over?"

"Twenty minutes," Mikhail said. "Hurry, pliz."

"It would go faster if the rest of you would get down here," Cale said. "Plenty of room for a party."

"Stand by," Sara said.

Maia watched in amazement as an icy derrick rose from the bow of the *Atlanta Nights*, shaping itself into something resembling a . . . water slide. It formed a thick, sloped platform that was angled to direct anything upon it onto the slide. The *Clara* moved to hover over the platform, Mikhail putting on a supreme display of piloting skill as he brought the 'copter down close to the icy platform Sara had created, perhaps with Harry's help.

Tanya, Burleigh, and Harry jumped down onto the icy platform and slid down on their rumps to the *Atlanta Nights*' deck. Maia caught each of them as they reached the bottom so they wouldn't go tumbling. Harry redirected the ice from the slide over the side of the ship, breaking it apart into small enough pieces that they couldn't damage the hull. "What about Snowball and Simulcast?" Maia asked.

"Prerogative of command," Tanya said as she shook herself like a wet dog. "The commander stays warm and dry while we are cold and wet."

"It ain't *that* warm or dry up there with the door open," Burleigh said. "And it takes two to run the sling for the ship's crew. We can't exactly slide them uphill."

"Spread out," Cale said. "Let's get these people to safety. Burleigh and Maia check the cabins. Tanya and Harry check below decks. I'll scan the top deck and check around the hull. Look alive, people, we've only got fifteen minutes before we've got to get out of here."

Burleigh looked at Maia with a smile, and the two of them trotted along the walkway to the building housing the crew section and bridge. The *Atlanta Nights* listed sharply to one side and then the other as a wave passed beneath it. Maia had to grab a railing to keep from being thrown overboard. For a moment when she looked over the railing, she saw nothing but a mountain of water as the wave receded.

"This storm's for real," Burleigh shouted over the storm. "This tub's not gonna last another half an hour in these seas. The captain ought to be brought up on charges for taking it out into the ocean."

"If we find him, you can write him a ticket, yeah?" Maia said.

Burleigh laughed.

They entered the bridge castle and began working their way through it, methodically but quickly. Maia checked doors on the left and Burleigh those on the right. They each called out "Hello?" regularly, in case someone wasn't able to move for some reason. They found crew cabins without any crew. The mess looked like the crew had been mid-meal. Plates of food had slid across the table and cups spilled on the floor. Cabinets that hadn't been lashed shut hung open, spilling their contents across counters and the floor.

"Geez," Maia said, looking at the debris. "Looks like they left in a hurry."

"A fire would do that." Burleigh pulled a radio from his pocket. "Snowcat and Devilfish reporting there's nobody here. We're gonna check the bridge."

"Copy that," Sara said. "You've got ten minutes. Reindeer, Igloo, anything?"

"Cargo's still here," Harry said over the radio. "Looks like it's dry refrigerated. Power's out down below decks. Emergency lighting only. They have a pretty full load. Probably a pretty lucrative haul. We're heading aft to the engine room."

"No crew here," Tanya added. "This does not feel right to me."

"No sign of exterior damage," Cale called. "Main deck cargo is still secure. Nobody moving up here. Also, it's really damn windy."

Burleigh stuck his head in to look at the bridge, cursed under his breath, then told Maia to join him. She was afraid he'd found a body. She didn't think she was ready for that part of the job just yet, but she nerved up and followed him onto the bridge.

The windows were smashed in. Rain and sea spray blasted through the broken glass. A couple control panels were blackened, as if they'd also suffered a fire. All the controls and gauges were dark. Maia pointed at a black spot on the bulkhead with dark radial burn lines spreading from it. "What's that?"

Burleigh looked at it. "Kind of looks like someone shot a flare gun in here." He scanned the floor and then stepped through the puddles to pick up an orange object, burned at its mouth. "Yeah, here it is."

"Why would someone shoot a flare gun inside?" Maia asked.

"No idea. Maybe it went off accidentally?"

"Does that even happen?"

Burleigh shrugged. "I don't know, but I can't think of any reason why someone would do it otherwise."

"Where's the crew?" Maia asked, not expecting anyone would have an immediate answer.

"The lifeboats are still moored," Cale said. "However they left, it wasn't that way."

A moment later, Tanya reported the engine room was vacant of crew, just like the rest of the ship. "The fire is out," she said. "But it looks like it was bad. The engine is badly burned. A total loss, I think."

"I wish we had a fucking psi who could maybe tell us what happened," Sara said over the radio. "Maybe everyone decided to take a swim at the same time. There's no way we're going to find them in this storm. Everyone get back up to the deck. Mikhail's going to bring the *Clara* down low for you to board and then it's asses and elbows back home."

"Something's wrong," Maia said to Burleigh as they descended from the bridge. "Why would everyone be gone? They called for help. Does somebody else have a helicopter that got here first? Or another boat?"

Burleigh shrugged, the motion making the head of his axe move up and down behind him. "No idea, kid. Maybe so, but it would have been nice to get the call before we came all the way out here."

The wind had picked up and everyone huddled together against it as the *Clara* dipped lower toward the deck. Maia watched its descent, nervous about Mikhail's ability to keep the helicopter under control.

Sara leaned out of the open side door, a safety strap keeping her from falling. She extended her arms and formed a platform of ice on the deck with a raised railing around the edges.

Harry reshaped it further, roughening the platform's base so it wouldn't be slippery as an ice rink. "All aboard," he shouted over the din of the 'copter overhead. Maia figured they were going to use the platform as an elevator to raise the group up to the 'copter instead of bringing them aboard one at a time using the cable sling. That didn't seem particularly safe, but then, nothing seemed safe with a hurricane barreling in toward them. She and the others stepped onto the platform and braced themselves.

The *Atlanta Nights* listed sideways suddenly as it slipped into a trough between waves. Mikhail lowered the *Clara* to compensate for the ship's drift, and then everything went wrong.

Chapter Six

*From Maia's playlist: "Always Crashing in
the Same Car" - David Bowie*

The crane derrick on the *Atlanta Nights*' bow, weakened by the abnormally rough motions of the boat, broke free and swung around like a batter drilling a fastball. The end of the crane smashed into the *Clara*'s tail section, shattering the stabilization rotor and swinging the 'copter around like it was a toy on the end of a string.

Sara and Michelle both flew out of the open door. The strap holding Sara jerked her back but Michelle hadn't been restrained, and she shot out past the deck toward the water, shrieking in terror. The nose of the 'copter crumpled into the deck and the rotors shattered into razor-sharp shrapnel. Maia screamed belatedly as a piece of metal flew at her face, only to be deflected away by Burleigh's titanium axe and stick itself into the deck like a lawn dart. "Go get Michelle!" he shouted over the sound of the helicopter dying its horrible mechanical death. He raised his axe and ran toward the wreck, presumably to try to save Sara and Mikhail.

Swimming was something Maia could do. She ran past the 'copter, which already had flames spreading from the engine compartment, and dove over the side where she'd last seen Michelle.

The choppy sea immediately dashed her against the *Atlanta Nights*' hull hard enough to make her see stars and nearly inhale a lungful of seawater. "Michelle!" she screamed. With the waves battering her and the rain driving seemingly in all directions, she couldn't see where the woman might be. She took a deep breath and dove below the surface.

It took her eyes a few seconds to adjust to the change in ambient light, but even though the sea was dark thanks to the ominous clouds overhead, she could still see shapes and shadows in the choppy water. The *Atlanta Nights* loomed large to one side, and off to the other was an irregular twist of limbs that could only be Michelle, sinking into the depths.

Maia flexed her arms and legs and raced through the water toward her teammate. The woman's eyes were shut and her jaw hung open. Maia guessed she'd probably gotten knocked out when she hit the water. She wrapped one arm around the unconscious woman and made for the surface. Their heads broke through a moment later and Maia took a moment to turn Michelle around to face her. "Michelle! Michelle! Can you hear me?"

Michelle didn't respond, and Maia knew she only had seconds to act. Swimming while keeping a deadweight passenger aloft wasn't easy, even with her enhanced strength. Her speed slowed to an awkward crawl. She felt Michelle's waterlogged weight threatening to drag her below the surface every second as she clawed and fought her way toward the ladder on the *Atlanta Nights'* side. It seemed like every time she got close, a wave would separate her from the boat, keeping it just out of reach. The rain and seawater splashing her face mixed with tears of frustration as once more she just missed grabbing the ladder.

At last, she managed to catch it with her fingertips and pulled herself close, using her parahuman strength to keep tight hold of the ladder with one hand. She moved Michelle into an awkward fireman's carry, as she would need two hands to ascend the ladder and couldn't risk dropping Michelle back into the ocean. Michelle's body bumped against her shoulders as she climbed and reached the deck in a few seconds.

The deck was a catastrophe.

The helicopter's fuel had ignited and the wreck was burning bright and hot in defiance of the storm. The fire had consumed part of the deck and smoke poured from a container that had been damaged when the main rotors hit it. The fire roared as loud as the wind as the rest of the team struggled to rescue the injured. Harry and Tanya were hunched over Sarah, who lay flat on the deck, while Cale fought to carry Mikhail to safety. The pilot's skin was charred and his clothes smoldered. Burleigh winced at the burns on his face and hands. Maia realized he must have used his axe to break apart the helicopter's cabin to pull Mikhail from the burning wreckage.

Maia realized suddenly that there was nobody to help her with Michelle. She had to try resuscitating the woman herself. She'd had emergency medical training at the Academy—everyone in Just Cause had to get certified and recertified time and time again. She tried to remember what to do first but her mind had gone blank.

Breathe, she thought. She had to get Michelle breathing again. She turned the woman's head and a bit of water leaked out from her mouth. That was a start. She checked to see if Michelle was breathing but with the boat swaying and the rain pelting, it nearly impossible to determine anything. The woman had gone pale and Maia was pretty sure she wasn't breathing at all.

She inhaled deeply, pinched Michelle's nose shut, and blew into her mouth—not a full power breath from her tremendous lung capacity, but a sustained pressure that made Michelle's chest expand a couple inches. She repeated the respiration process and checked again. Still nothing. Maia checked for a pulse but again, the environment made it nearly impossible to determine if her heart was beating or not. She clasped her wrist, placed her other palm on the woman's chest, and compressed it, careful to use only a fraction of her strength the way she'd been taught at the Academy.

She remembered the speed, because it was the same as one of her favorite songs by Queen, unfortunately called *Another One Bites the Dust*. She muttered it under her breath as she counted out thirty compressions, then blew twice into Michelle's mouth.

Cale flew across the deck to land beside Maia. "You compress, I'll breathe."

Maia nodded and began another round of compressions. "What about . . . Mikhail?"

Cale shook his head.

"Twenty-nine . . . thirty. Breathe!"

Cale blew two lungfuls of air into Michelle, then gasped. "Go."

Maia started the next round of chest compressions. She felt something crack beneath her hand and had a horrible thought that she'd just broken one of Michelle's ribs. She kept going.

Michelle coughed suddenly and sprayed seawater-diluted vomit to one side, narrowly missing Cale. He grimaced, turned her head, and wiped out her mouth.

"Breathe!" Maia said. Even with her super-strength, she was tiring out from the strain of trying to save Michelle's life.

Cale bent, but Michelle coughed again and more water came out. She raised a hand to grab onto Cale's arm and made a husky groaning sound. "Are you hurt?" Cale asked.

Michelle's eyelids fluttered and for a moment, Maia thought she was going to go under and they'd have to start CPR again, but then her face twisted into a wince of pain. "Chest . . . hurts to breathe . . ."

Cale turned to Maia. "Be gentle, but get her into a cabin and out of this rain."

"Okay." Maia carefully slid her arms under Michelle, who groaned in pain as she was jostled.

"Good job, Maia. You saved her life today." Cale wiped rain from his face. "Get her settled and then help Burleigh. I've got to check on Sara."

Coughs wracked Michelle, and she cried out in pain as her damaged ribs moved in an uncomfortable way. More water dribbled from her mouth. "Sorry," Maia said. "I know you're hurt."

Michelle winced. "I-it's . . . okay. I'm . . . alive."

Maia opened the first cabin door she came to and found a small dorm room-style berth with two twin beds. The room was dark, with only a single porthole allowing any light in at all. Lightning flickered outside and the answering peal of thunder came almost immediately. Michelle quaked with uncontrollable shivers. Maia knew she needed to get the wet clothing off her teammate before hypothermia set in. There were blankets on the beds and Michelle could warm up so long as she stayed dry. "I've got to get you undressed," Maia said. "It's going to hurt, yeah?"

Michelle nodded. "Do it."

Maia tugged the Velcro seal open and pulled down the zipper beneath. Michelle's soaked red coveralls came away to reveal a second, skintight bodysuit beneath, quilted with insulating material and lined with battery-powered thermal wires. Maia checked Michelle's suit liner. The collar, wrists, and ankles were all wet from her plunge, but the rest of the suit seemed to be mostly dry. She found the belt switch to activate the suit heater and turned it on. Michelle hissed and groaned with the pain but between the two of them, they got her laid out with her feet elevated and covered with two blankets and a quilt. She hoped there would be enough blankets for Sara and . . .

It hit her that they wouldn't need them for Mikhail, and she burst into tears.

The risk of death, either to comrades or innocent bystanders, was an expected occurrence for any working superhero. Being a superhero was a dangerous occupation in the best of times, and most of them expected to die with their boots on. Maia had not personally experienced death of anyone around her, something which she had taken for granted. She hadn't known Mikhail at all; she hadn't even gotten to meet him before boarding the *Clara*, and now she never would.

Burleigh stepped into the cabin, ducking through the small hatch, and put his arms around Maia. She shrank against his chest, sniffling. "Hey . . . it's okay. You're safe. You saved Michelle. You did good, kid."

"What about y-you?"

"I heal quick. It doesn't hurt any more. Well, not really." He grew sober. "Sara's hurt pretty bad, I think. She got jerked around at the end of her safety strap and hit the deck hard when the 'copter did. She's got a lot of broken bones and Harry thinks she's got pretty bad internal injuries."

"Is she g-going to die?" Maia wiped her eyes.

"I don't know," Burleigh admitted. "But it doesn't look too good."

"What about the rest of us? How bad are things?"

He shook his head. "Don't look too good for us either.'copter's gone, and we're adrift with a hurricane coming."

"It's not already here?"

"No, the worst hasn't hit us yet."

"What are we going to do?"

"I don't know."

Chapter Seven

From Maia's playlist: "Dust in the Wind" - Kansas

"We're in a hell of a spot," Cale said as he leaned against the bulkhead. He and Harry had brought Sara into the same cabin as Michelle. The tiny woman was unconscious and her face was swollen and bruised from smashing against the deck when the 'copter went down. She'd avoided the burns that had killed Mikhail and wounded Burleigh, but she looked like she'd taken a severe beating. Harry was the designated medic, but his expertise was primarily limited to stabilizing someone until they could be brought to real medical professionals.

"Not so much helpful to point out," Tanya said. She'd wrapped up Mikhail's body in a tarp and pulled it into the cabin so it wouldn't accidentally wash overboard in the rough sea. The *Atlanta Nights* continued its awkward listing, slipping sideways into the troughs between waves and nosing through the crests that broke over its deck. "Bilge is filling. We will sink soon if we do not get pumps working."

"That won't be easy after the fire in the engine room. Most of the batteries are shot and the wiring is flat out melted," Cale said. He'd gone down to illuminate the engine room and agreed with Tanya's assessment that it was a total loss. "I don't know if any of it is repairable."

"The crew must have tried that already, and they're not here, are they?" Harry said. "Did they all jump overboard in a . . . a suicide pact?"

"It's a mystery, but that doesn't help us now. We've got to either get off this ship or get it moving under its own power again," Cale said. "Otherwise, Tanya is right. We're going to be swamped if we can't get the power restored. I know none of us are particularly nautical, but there are some basic things we can check. Maybe there's a generator stowed somewhere for emergencies so we can get the bilge pumps and radio working."

"I kind of think they would already have tried that, yeah?" Maia said.

"It still doesn't hurt to check. Otherwise, we can take one of the lifeboats," Cale said.

"Sara's in a bad way," Harry said. "If we can't get her some kind of real medical attention soon . . ." He didn't finish his statement, but he didn't have to. Everyone could see how bad her injuries were.

"How are you feeling, Michelle?" Maia asked. She was so scared she had to keep her arms tightly folded so her hands wouldn't shake and give her away. Even so, she had a quaver in her voice she couldn't hide no matter how hard she tried. They could train and train at session after session at the Academy and still run into a completely unfamiliar situation, which is what had happened.

"Like Burleigh . . . jumped on me," Michelle coughed.

"Hey, I was all the way over there," Burleigh said, pointing toward the bow. "If I'd been the one doin' the jumpin', I'm pretty sure you'd resemble roadkill by now."

"Any chance you can raise anyone to come to our aid?" Cale asked Michelle.

She shook her head and winced. "I can't . . . focus."

"Maybe you ought to fly back to Deadhorse," Harry said. "Bring help. The Coast Guard."

Cale shook his head. "Even if I left right now and found someone right away, it would be four hours before anyone could get back out here. This ship isn't going to still be afloat in four hours. And as honorable as everyone is up here on top of the world, there's not a pilot out there who would fly into this storm."

"At least, not a sane one," Burleigh said under his breath. "Looks like we have to save ourselves then. What are your orders, boss?"

The *Atlanta Nights* swayed enough to spill some things off a shelf. Elsewhere in the ship, glass shattered, audible even over the whistle of the wind.

"I want a bridge-to-bilge search of this ship. Look for anything that can help us survive the storm. I need a volunteer to stay here with the injured so they're not alone."

Maia raised her hand. "I'll stay."

Cale nodded. "Thank you, Maia."

"Thank you," Michelle whispered.

"Everyone be careful," Cale said. "But hurry. Back here in no more than ten minutes with whatever you find. If we can't save the ship, we're leaving on a lifeboat in fifteen."

Tanya pulled a flashlight from a costume pouch and vanished in a blur. Harry followed after, taking out his own flashlight. Cale was his own light and he departed next. Burleigh paused by the door. Lightning flashed and reflected off the head of his axe, still strapped to his back. "It's gonna be okay, kid, don't worry."

"I'm not worried," Maia lied.

* * *

The team reconvened in the cabin a few minutes later. Tanya had searched the entire lower deck and found nothing but cargo. "Is all packaged food," she said. "We will not starve, but we may not live long enough to worry about it."

"Typical Russian," Harry said. "I checked the sick bay. Found some good painkillers and injectables. And this is a treasure right here." He held up a plastic pill bottle and a large canteen. "Water purification tablets and a filtration canteen. We can make ten gallons of drinkable water out of seawater with this."

"So we will not be thirsty when we die," Tanya said.

Maia found her teammate's fatalism strangely cheering, as if the Russian's acceptance of certain death was denying it.

"There will be water on the lifeboat," Harry said. "But this means more if we need it."

"Assuming these yahoos maintained their lifeboats properly," Burleigh said. "I wouldn't put it past them to have let that slide. There's fuel leaking into the bilge and if the storm hadn't blown out the 'copter fire, we might have torched the entire ship by now. As it is, one good spark and we'll have ourselves a Viking funeral they might see all the way in Sweden."

"Are we that far away from Alaska?" Maia asked, and then wished she hadn't because of how naive it made her sound. She wished she had hair so she could bow her head and hide behind it. If she still had her hoodie, she could have used that, but it had burned in the helicopter wreck.

"No, but it's far enough we might as well be," Cale said. "I found a gas-powered generator. It looks like the crew started to get it set up to connect to the radio, but they didn't finish."

"Why would they leave if they had that?" Maia asked. "Their best chance would have been to stay here."

"I don't know," Cale said. "And I don't know how they left the ship unless they all jumped overboard. I can't explain it."

Brilliant lightning flashed through the cabin's porthole, overpowering Cale's soft glow. Instant thunder boomed and Burleigh yelped belatedly, jumping away from the bulkhead where he'd been leaning.

"What happened?" Maia asked.

"Got a shock." He rubbed his shoulder. "That one must've hit the ship." He winced at the momentary discomfort, and then froze. "Maia . . ." he whispered. "Don't move."

Maia felt her throat close up in fear. What had he seen? "What is it?" she whispered.

"Cale?" Burleigh's voice was barely audible over the roar of the storm. "You see it? I'm not just imagining it?"

"I see it," Cale said.

"I see it too," Tanya whispered.

Burleigh reached over his shoulder and pulled his axe from its straps.

"What is it?" Maia repeated. "Is it . . . a rat?" She'd heard ships had rats. She had never seen one before and thought they were probably just like big mice, but Burleigh was acting like it was something else.

Something worse.

"Maia . . ." Cale said softly. "When I say, step over to me as quick as you can. There's . . . something . . . on the ceiling. Harry, Tanya, get clear."

Something as cold as liquid nitrogen ran through Maia's veins. What was it? She was terrified to look, but the temptation to was almost overwhelming. She was the rookie, though, and her teammates were more experienced superheroes. Whatever it was, they were ready to handle it. Of course they were.

"Now," Cale said.

Maia took three quick steps to cross the cabin until she was against the far bulkhead where Cale was standing. Harry went one way while Tanya went the other as Burleigh whipped his axe upward to clang against the ceiling.

Something silvery the size of a cat fell to the floor, albeit with too many legs.

"Damn it!" Burleigh yelled as the thing skittered sideways underneath Michelle's bunk. "Cale!"

Cale dropped to the floor, shining his luminescence under the bed while Burleigh sprawled flat, axe ready to swing.

Tanya screamed and leaped across the room as the thing ran out from under the bunk, legs flying in a blur. Burleigh's swing caught the creature a glancing blow and it bounced off the bulkhead from the impact before racing through the open hatch.

"What the hell was that?" Harry shouted.

Maia saw what looked like a piece of metal twitching on the floor and she realized Burleigh had severed one of the thing's legs with his last blow. She steeled herself and bent to pick it up.

"Careful," Cale said. "We don't know what that is."

The leg was maybe ten inches long with a single joint in it like a spider's. It was smooth and metallic, but instead of a foot at the end, it had a fan of fine tendrils or tentacles. They twitched back and forth as if they had minds of their own. The end where Burleigh's axe had severed it was just sheared metal. There wasn't any kind of organic fluid leaking or mechanical wires or hydraulics. It looked as if someone had sliced through an aluminum dowel rod. As she looked at it, Maia got the sense that even though it was moving, it wasn't alive. Not in the sense that she and the others were, at any rate. "It's a machine, yeah," she declared, hoping her statement made it true. The idea of holding a piece of a machine felt far less oogie to her than holding a creature's leg. It stopped twitching after a few seconds, perhaps due to being disconnected from the main body, and became as inert as a stick.

"Never seen machine like that." Tanya's voice shook.

Maia tucked the leg into her pack for future examination. Whatever else it might have been, it seemed kind of high-tech and someone in Just Cause would certainly want to take a look at it when the team was safe.

"Is it a . . . a toy of some kind?" Harry asked. "Who would have a toy like that?"

"I don't know, and right now I don't care," Cale said. "It's gone, and whatever it is, it's not going to help us get out of our predicament."

As if to illustrate his point, *Atlanta Nights* tipped dangerously and seawater splashed against the porthole, coming above the deck. The ship groaned as its keel flexed in a way it hadn't been designed to.

Burleigh raised his head and sniffed. "We've gotta get out of here," he said. "I think the leakin' fuel's on fire."

"Where can we go?" Tanya cried. "We are in middle of ocean in storm!"

"Knock it off!" Cale shouted.

Tanya shut her mouth with an almost audible snap.

Cale lowered his head. "I'm sorry, I didn't mean to yell. Get Sara and Michelle into the starboard lifeboat, and hurry. With burning fuel, there won't be much left of this ship shortly."

Chapter Eight

From Maia's playlist: "Jump Into the Fire" - <u>Harry Nilsson</u>

The *Atlanta Nights*' stern was fully ablaze as the team emerged from the cabin back onto the swaying deck. The storm had intensified so much Maia couldn't believe it hadn't already put out the fire. She struggled to carry Michelle, not because she couldn't easily lift her teammate, but because she was trying so hard to keep from dropping her. The storm's rain had become sleet, and the stinging wind bit at them with the fury of a wild animal. The deck had grown slick and treacherous.

"This is nice," Harry yelled as he and Cale struggled to prepare the lifeboat.

Lightning forked across the sky and Maia saw something that made her stop short. She'd never seen a tornado in person, but she'd seen videos of them. A long, swirling rope of darkness stretched between the ocean and the spinning clouds overhead, only a few dozen yards away from the burning *Atlanta Nights*. "Look!" she screamed and pointed.

The waterspout didn't last more than a few seconds, but the dark clouds twisted in such a way as to suggest it could return at any moment.

Cale and Harry turned their frantic attention back to the lifeboat. They pulled the pins from the davit that would allow the boat to descend once the brake was released, then gave each other a thumbs-up. "Okay, all aboard," Cale said. "Let's get away from this floating deathtrap."

The lifeboat looked more like a submarine than a boat. It was a giant orange lozenge with a raised pilot's cabin at the stern, completely enclosed. At least they would be dry inside it, Maia thought, so long as the crew had maintained the lifeboat properly. That raised another question in her mind. There was another lifeboat on the port side. Neither one had been released and the crew was still missing, as if they'd all jumped overboard. It made the back of her neck tickle, as if she were being watched. The heat from the burning fuel made her face prickle as she helped Michelle into the lifeboat. The woman winced from the pain of her broken ribs as Maia got her strapped into one of the cramped seats. "All good, yeah?"

Michelle coughed and grimaced. "I'll live, probably."

The center line of the boat was taken up by its frame and support structure, leaving the passengers the cramped space around the edges. Maia turned back to the hatch and Burleigh handed Sara to her. The woman felt fragile in her hands, and groaned as the swaying boat jostled her. Since the lifeboat was designed to hold some fifteen people, Maia gave Sara enough room to lay on the seats. She improvised with the straps until she got Sara immobilized so she wouldn't be at risk of falling in the rough seas.

Tanya slipped inside, followed by Harry and Burleigh. The big man had a tough time squeezing himself through the hatch. Wind whipped around Cale as he was the last to enter, driving sleet against him hard enough to cut his face through his mask. He dogged the hatch shut and climbed into the pilot's chair, which sat up high enough that he'd be able to see through the upper windows over the boat's hull. He pulled his hood and cowl back so he could see unimpeded. A crimson streak on one cheek showed where sleet had cut him. The release lever was so obvious that even Maia could have guessed which one it was. "Everyone ready?"

A chorus of affirmatives followed.

"Hold on," Cale said. "Here we go. This is going to be a little exciting." He yanked the lever and Maia's stomach leaped into her throat as the lifeboat dropped in free fall. The fall might have only lasted a second, but it felt like an eternity, followed by a terrifying impact as the boat splashed into the ocean. Water dashed against the portholes. For a moment, she thought they were sinking, but then the boat righted itself and popped back up to the surface like a cork.

The storm caught it immediately and dashed it through a huge wave, followed by sliding it sideways into a trough where sleet battered against it. Maia screamed as the boat spun around, beaten by more waves. She wanted to run, but there was nowhere to run. She wanted to swim away, but that would mean leaving everyone else behind and then she would be all alone. She squeezed her eyes shut, afraid to look at anything, but then opened them a second later, terrified at missing something crucial to their survival. Cale fought the small steering wheel, trying to get some semblance of control. "Come on . . . come on . . ." He kicked a floor panel aside to reveal a small blue engine. "Somebody find out why the engine isn't starting!" he shouted over the din of waves and wind and Tanya retching on an empty stomach from the twisting motion of the boat.

Burleigh unstrapped himself and hunched over to look. "I need a light. Not yours, Cale."

Maia realized that was something she could do. She didn't have to be helpless. She could be *useful*. She handed him the flashlight from her pack. Her fingers brushed against the severed mechanical spider thing's leg that she'd taken from the *Atlanta Nights*. It had curled up tightly against itself, the way a real spider's legs would when it died. Maybe it had some residual power when it had been severed, and the curling inside Maia's pack had been its last motion.

"Got it!" Burleigh said. "Battery wasn't connected. Thanks, kid." He replaced the engine cover and handed the flashlight back to Maia. "These things ought to come with an instruction manual."

Cale dropped something onto the engine cover. Maia shined her flashlight on it. It was a booklet. *Marine Survival 3rd Edition.* Burleigh laughed sharply, as if he were giving their situation the finger. Beneath Cale's feet, the Diesel engine rumbled to life. "Now we're getting somewhere," he said. "Let's hope that crew of idiots was smart enough to keep their lifeboat fully stocked and fueled."

"Where are we headin', boss?" Burleigh asked.

"No idea, Burleigh. This pokey little engine isn't powerful enough to fight these waves, and a compass isn't going to do us much good this far north."

"So we don't know where we're going, yeah?" Maia asked.

"But we're makin' great time," Burleigh said with a laugh. The lifeboat tilted far forward as a wave caught it from behind. It crashed nose-first into the trough at the bottom, flinging him against the forward bulkhead. "Ow!" he yelped.

"Burleigh!" Maia cried and reached for her straps.

"Don't unstrap. That's an order, Maia," Cale said. "Sorry. Burleigh, you all right?"

"I'll live," Burleigh grumbled. "But don't ask me to move anytime soon. I'm wedged in up here pretty good."

"Grow . . . smaller," came Sara's weak voice.

"Sara!" Tanya seemed to have found an equilibrium with her motion sickness and although she still clutched a bag in one hand, she didn't appear to have needed it. She reached out and took Sara's hand.

Sara coughed and dark flecks of blood splattered the bench beside her. "How are . . . we doing?"

"We're alive," Cale said. "Except for Mikhail. We couldn't find anyone on the *Atlanta Nights*. We're in its lifeboat."

"Stupid name . . . for a . . . fucking boat." Sara closed her eyes.

"Snowball? Sara? *Sara?*" Sara didn't respond. Tanya pulled off one of her gloves to check for a pulse on their leader.

Harry undid his straps and moved gingerly around the central supports to kneel down next to Sara. "Sara?" He put the back of his hand against her nose. "She's not breathing!"

A wave crashed beneath the lifeboat, flinging its bow into the air. Harry tumbled back to the aft bulkhead. Burleigh's axe slipped out of its straps and whirled through the lifeboat cabin. Maia reached out and grabbed the haft just before the titanium head could bury itself in Harry's face. She handed it to Michelle. "Hold this." She released her own straps.

"You all need to strap back in right now," Cale shouted. "The sea is getting rougher."

"But Sara!" Harry shouted back, and crawled back along the bulkhead to kneel beside her once more. Maia wriggled through the cramped space to join him.

There was no room to effectively perform CPR on Sara, but Harry and Maia made an effort to do so. Working on her was like working on the child dummy Maia remembered from her first-aid training. She was so small, and fragile, and her chest was . . . mushy. "Harry . . ."

"No, she can't be! We have to try!" he shouted.

The lifeboat hurtled sideways and Harry's head bounced off the seat beside Sara. He winced and rubbed the spot on his scalp over his right ear. Fresh blood dribbled down his cheek from the cut.

"Harry, I think she's gone. Her ribs . . . they're all broken already. She's probably got too much trauma, yeah?" She reached out to touch his arm.

"But we could still . . ."

"Harry, CPR will not fix crushed chest and organs," Tanya said. "She is not like Burleigh. She does not heal."

"She needed a hospital and a trauma team," Cale said from the pilot's seat. "I know you tried. We all tried, but we don't have time to mourn if we're going to survive this."

"That's cold-blooded, Cale," Harry shouted. "Who died and made you God?"

"Snowball did," Michelle said, wheezing through lungs that were still irritated from her near -drowning. She managed to cough out, "He's in command now."

Those four simple words took the wind out of Harry's sails and he slumped beside Sara's body. "Goddammit." He wiped his eyes. "This isn't how we're supposed to go. She died for nothing. Nothing."

Maia burst into tears. Just like Mikhail, she hadn't had a chance to get to know Sara, and now she never would. "I'm sorry," she said to Harry. "I'm sorry to all of you . . ."

"Hey, don't apologize," Burleigh said as he extricated himself from the cramped bow. "None of this is your fault. It's not anybody's fault. We came here to do what we signed on for. Search and rescue. Just because we didn't find nobody to rescue don't mean we shouldn't have come. It's only failin' if we don't try." He had to turn himself sideways to fit around the support beam at the lifeboat's bow.

"Someone will have to rescue us, Snowcat," Tanya said. "I do not like our chances."

"At least one of us is back to normal," Burleigh smiled at Tanya. "Cale how's it looking?"

The lifeboat flew off the top of a wave and crashed down hard enough to send Burleigh crashing back into the bow bulkhead once more. He bellowed in discomfort.

"Like shit," Cale said.

"We need to find land," Harry said.

"How about sea ice?" Cale asked.

"Sea ice? Where?" Harry asked.

"In the sea, stupid," Michelle said, and broke out coughing again.

Harry ignored his teammate's dig and climbed up to peek through the pilot windows. "Yeah. Yeah, I can work with that." He raised a hand but then stopped. "Shit. I can't work through the glass. I've got to be in open air."

"Maia, undo a couple of the spare harnesses," Cale said. "We need to make a couple of safety lines. I won't have anyone getting thrown off the top of the lifeboat."

"Open that hatch and we will take on much water," Tanya said.

"Then I guess you better find a bucket," Burleigh said, wrestling himself free of the bow again.

"Why two harnesses?" Harry asked.

"Maia's going up top with you."

"I am?" Maia's eyes widened. "In the *hurricane*?"

"If Harry goes overboard, you're the only one who can save him," Cale said.

"I only need a couple of minutes to get us onto that floe," Harry said, shrugging his shoulders into a safety harness and clipping the carabiner to his waist.

"What will that accomplish?" Tanya burped and opened her vomit bag but refrained from using it.

"Maybe it'll keep us from dying. I can make a shelter and we can ride out the storm without being tossed around like we are now." Harry checked the harness holding him. He had enough slack that he could stick his head and shoulders up through the top hatch. Maia would stand right behind him, supporting him and keeping hold of him as a second layer of security. "Unless someone has any better ideas."

"You sure you're up for it, Harry?" Burleigh asked.

"I have to be," Harry said, tightening the straps a bit more. "Sara wouldn't want any of us to quit." He paused. "Sorry, everyone. It's going to get cold and wet in here."

Burleigh held up a bucket. "Bring it, brother."

Harry opened the top hatch and several gallons of icy ocean water immediately poured in, drenching him and Maia. Sleet splattered against both of them, driving with the force of hailstones in the angry wind. Thunder roared and a constant barrage of lightning flashed overhead, occasionally sending questing fingers to strike breaking waves. Maia gasped as she saw another waterspout dancing across the ocean, bigger and meaner-looking than the small one that had briefly appeared during their escape from the *Atlanta Nights*. The lifeboat spun through a trough between waves.

"Harry, are you all right?" Maia called in his ear.

He didn't reply.

"*Harry!*"

He jumped. "Sorry, I'm trying to find the ice. I saw it a minute ago. Did we get blown away from it?"

"Whatever you do, you better do it quick. That tornado thing is getting closer."

A wave lifted the lifeboat, tilting it sideways and sending another torrent of water in through the open hatch.

"You guys don't hurry, we are gonna sink," Burleigh shouted. "There's a lot of water in here." The fear in his voice was real, and Maia knew it was because he couldn't swim. If the lifeboat capsized, it wouldn't matter if any of them could swim. Maia couldn't save all of them before they drowned, and even if she could, there would be nowhere safe to go.

Maia spotted an expanse of white off to the right and pointed it out to Harry. "There it is! Can you get it closer to us?"

A monster wave, driven by the waterspout, lifted the lifeboat dozens of feet above the prevailing surface level and the plain of ice spread out beneath them. Harry said, "I don't think that's going to be a problem."

Chapter Nine

From Maia's playlist: "Burn / Stormbringer" - Whitesnake

As the giant waterspout-driven wave crested and the lifeboat tilted downward, Maia expected them to be dashed against the icy plain. She wanted to shut her eyes so she wouldn't have to see their impending deaths approaching, but a sick fascination with the process kept her watching. The wave crashed down, sending salt water coursing across the ice, but a wave of moving ice rose upward, catching their tumble on its own crest. Harry yelled wordlessly as he channeled his power into the ice beneath them.

The ice wave narrowed and lengthened, forming itself into less of a hill and more of a half-pipe like a bobsled course. The icy walls closed in around the sliding lifeboat, guiding it further away from the shoreline as well as keeping it upright. Wind whistled around Harry and Maia as the boat slid along the incline. At last, the vessel's momentum slowed and it ground to a halt along a patch of icy gravel. Harry slumped forward against the hatch and Maia squeezed him. "You did it!" she whispered in his ear.

"One . . . more . . . thing," Harry said, and raised his shaking arms again. "Help me."

From behind him, Maia helped steady Harry's arms. The man was clearly exhausted but still had enough gas in the tank to reshape the nearby ice into a dome surrounding the lifeboat, coming all the way up to the top of the hull. From what Maia could see, they would be able to exit through one of the side hatches and be underneath the dome, which would deflect the wind and protect them from any waves that made it so far inland as they had come.

Harry went limp and Maia carefully lowered him inside the lifeboat, closing the hatch behind them. "We're down, and we're safe for the moment, yeah," she said.

"Safe is relative term," Tanya said. She had drawn her feet up onto the seat, as six inches of seawater filled the lifeboat's bilge.

"You okay, kid?" Burleigh asked her.

"Yeah, but Harry's burned out." He was, in fact, completely unconscious and she was more carrying him than supporting him. She laid him down across the seats. Tanya covered him with a blanket from the lifeboat stores. Someone had wrapped a tarp or poncho or something similar around Sara's body. It brought a lump to Maia's throat as it finally hit her that the woman was dead. "Fuck," she said softly, because that's what Sara would have said.

"What do we do now?" Tanya asked.

"We rest, heal, and wait for the storm to blow over. Arctic storms don't last long. Give it a few hours and we'll be past the worst of it. Then we can either use the lifeboat radio to call for help or Michelle can do it, if she's up for it." Cale climbed down from the pilot's seat to sit beside Michelle. "How are you feeling?"

"Can't hardly breathe." Michelle winced with the extra effort of speaking.

"Anybody mind if I step outside?" Burleigh asked. "I've, uh, gotta take a leak."

Maia raised her hand. "Me too, actually. Maybe we could sit outside, too. There's more room and the cold doesn't bother us, yeah?"

Cale nodded. "Let's not be gross about it. Latrine is on the port side. One at a time, please. Everyone gets a chance to go."

Maia and Burleigh took an insulating blanket outside with them, not because they were worried about the cold, but so they wouldn't have to get wet sitting on the ice.

Burleigh trotted around to the far side of the lifeboat and returned a minute later, looking relieved and much more cheerful. "Facilities leave a bit to be desired," he said. "I didn't leave a tip for the attendant."

Maia went around to the far side of the lifeboat herself and found what she assumed was a good spot. Not that any particular place was better than any other. If she'd been wearing an actual wetsuit, she'd have had to completely peel herself out of it in order to pee. Fortunately, the Just Cause costume department had perfected removable flaps and patches that allowed heroes to take care of their personal business conveniently. Maia had never been camping thanks to her fosters who had felt keeping her locked up was more important, so it was actually the first time as an adult she'd ever not peed in a toilet. It felt weird and, strangely, a little freeing. She kicked a little loose snow over the hole she'd made and resealed her costume.

Burleigh had unfolded the blanket and was lying on it with his hands behind his head, his axe on the ice beside him, and his eyes closed. He looked like he was already asleep, but he popped one eye open as she approached. "Plenty of room if you don't wanna stretch out on the ice, kid."

"You keep calling me that." Maia sat beside him and took a deep breath, letting the cold air fill her lungs and rejuvenate her. She could hear the storm howling outside the ice dome but the air was still and dry within it. It was almost peaceful.

"I can stop if you don't like it. I can just call you Maia, or Devilfish, or *hey you*. I'm easy."

"No . . . I do like it. I never had a real nickname before. That's different than a superhero name, yeah? You can pick your own superhero name, but other people give you a nickname. Other people only ever called me mean names before now." She smiled at Burleigh. "You gave me my first *real* nickname, and I like it."

"I'm sorry people haven't been nice to you. People are assholes. I seen plenty of it in my life, both as a black man and a para. You're lucky to be up here on the top of the world with the rest of us. Nobody's got time to be an asshole, and you don't want to be an asshole to someone else because that guy might be the one who can save your life in an accident." Burleigh closed his eyes again.

"Life is too short to be asshole," Tanya said as she trotted around from the far side of the lifeboat. "Can I sit with you? I feel claustrophobic inside boat."

Maia scooted over to make room for Tanya on the blanket between her and Burleigh. "Sure, just don't be an asshole, yeah?"

Tanya and Burleigh snickered at that, and Maia felt her heart grow warm.

Tanya offered wrapped food bars of some kind to each of them. "Cale says these are nutrient-dense. Will help rejuvenate you."

"Thanks, yeah," Maia said, and accepted one.

"Do not thank me before you taste it."

Burleigh smiled without opening his eyes. "They ain't that bad. Taste kind of like cookies . . . if you got a real good imagination."

Maia ate the bar in silence, listening to the wail of the wind outside the ice dome and the sandblasting of sleet and ice crystals against it. The bar wasn't nearly as bad as Tanya had intimated. As Burleigh said, it did taste very much like a coconut cookie.

"What will happen to us after we are rescued?" Tanya asked into the quiet. Burleigh jumped a little at the sound of her voice; he must have just drifted off to sleep. "We have lost our leader. We have failed to rescue civilians. We ourselves must be rescued."

"I don't think it's as bad as that, yeah?" Maia tucked the wrapper from her bar into her pouch. "This is a dangerous part of the world and a dangerous job. They're not going to . . . to fire us."

"You, perhaps not. Me, they may send back to Russia." Tanya pulled her knees up to her chest and hugged them. "I do not want to go."

"Why not?" Maia asked. "You don't want to see your family?"

"Very much so, I do, but they are in danger because of me."

"How so?" Burleigh sat up, apparently deciding sleep was not going to happen.

"I am a . . . tool of my government. I must do as I am told, or my family will be punished. It is how Russia keeps its parahumans under control. Here, in America, you have a choice. If you choose to leave Just Cause, you are free to do so. I am here because my government ordered it. If I am discharged, I must go to work for Russian government, doing dirty work in private and being a . . . a suck-up in public. This is how Russia is."

"I'm sorry. That's terrible." Maia put her arm around Tanya.

Tanya spat onto the ice. "Putin is piece of shit, and I am only safe saying so here where nobody can hear it. They poison critics and defectors. They have psionic assassins. Many secret parahumans work for government."

"Scary stuff," Burleigh said. "Makes you all the braver for bein' here. I'm impressed, and it takes a lot to impress me." He leaned back and put his hands behind his head once more. His eyes focused on the ice overhead. "What the hell's that?"

Chapter Ten

From Maia's playlist: "Stand and Fight" - James Taylor

A shadow moved across the surface of the ice overhead, slowly and deliberately, but a shadow nonetheless. It was twilight-dark beneath the storm clouds and blowing sleet, but against the white ice, the shadow, although indistinct, was clearly a moving figure of some kind.

"Could it be a bird?" Maia asked.

"No bird would fly in this weather," Tanya said. "It is too small for a caribou. Perhaps a fox or rabbit."

An image of metallic legs scrabbling across the hull came unbidden to Maia's mind. "I hope it's not one of those spider things, yeah?"

Burleigh frowned. "I wish you hadn't said that."

Another shadow joined the first in its methodical traverse of the ice dome. Then a third joined them.

"I *really* wish you hadn't said that," Burleigh said. He turned to the lifeboat. "Cale, can you see anything out of the pilot windows?"

Cale appeared at the hatch. "No, the windows are iced over. What's up?"

"Something's out there."

Cale looked up at the dome, then lit himself up like a floodlight. The shadows froze at the sudden illumination, but the ice dome was too thick to see anything more than shapeless dark blobs. At first, Maia thought there were only three, but as she turned around slowly, she saw there were more.

81

A lot more.

She remembered that dead mechanical leg, curled up in her pouch. She hoped it hadn't been the reason the things were coming after them. What if she had doomed everyone on the team with a foolish, rookie mistake? She thought about throwing it away, but if it was the reason the things had come, tossing it aside wouldn't make a difference. On the other hand, it might possibly be useful at some point in the future. The leg would stay where it was for the time being.

"Tanya, get back in here and check for an Epi-pen in the first aid kit. If there is one, give it to Michelle. Michelle, I want you ready to hit Harry with it," Cale said. "But not unless I give the order."

"*Da*," Tanya said and trotted back to the side hatch.

A weak cough confirmed Michelle's understanding of the order.

"What's that noise?" Maia asked, hearing something unpleasant from the dome overhead.

Everyone went silent.

The unmistakable sound of scratching on the ice dome was like fingernails on a chalkboard, the way it sent nervous shivers down between Maia's shoulder blades. "They're trying to get in," Burleigh said. "They know we're in here."

"Maia, Burleigh, back on board the lifeboat now," Cale said.

Maia and Burleigh glanced at each other, then ran to the side hatch. They squeezed through it and Burleigh closed it tight behind them.

Inside the lifeboat, they heard the tinny sound of tiny metallic feet clacking across the hull.

"What are they? What do they want?" Tanya sounded afraid and Maia couldn't blame her.

"I don't know what they are, but I think they want us," Cale said.

"For what?"

"Believe me, I wish I knew."

"I don't like it in here, boss," Burleigh said. "It's crowded and cramped and there's no room to fight if we have to. I like our odds better out on the ice."

Cale's laugh was sharp and humorless. "I don't."

A shrieking, grinding whine filled the cabin interior, making all of them wince and clap their hands over their ears. "What is that?" Tanya shouted over the din.

"Drilling," Burleigh replied. "They're trying to cut through the hull."

"We've got to get them off," Cale shouted. "We need this boat to stay seaworthy!"

Burleigh looked at Maia. "Come on, kid. Let's go stomp some spiders."

Maia glanced around. She'd been terrible in parahuman combat classes at the Academy. She got nervous. She froze.

Fighting robot spiders at the top of the world hadn't even been close to something she'd imagined.

"I, uh, need a weapon, yeah?" If the spiders were as small and fast as the one they'd found in the *Atlanta Nights*, a weapon would be imperative to even the odds.

Michelle pushed a hardwood stick with an end that looked like a combination hook and blunt spear point at her. She took it. "What's this?"

"Boat hook," Cale said. "Unless you want a hatchet."

"No, I'll leave the chopping stuff to the expert." Maia nodded toward Burleigh, who gripped his axe in one hand and looked eager to start swinging it.

"All right." Cale picked up a flare gun. "You two get out there. Tanya, you're on reserve if they need backup. Michelle, take charge of the adrenaline syringe. If we need Harry, make sure he's ready to fight."

Maia reached the bottom of the ladder to the top hatch and realized her hands were shaking. "Um . . . I'm not . . ."

Burleigh put a heavy hand on her shoulder. "Don't worry, kid, I'll watch your back. You just watch where you swing that stick."

"Maybe you should go first, yeah?"

"I would love to, but I'm so big it'll take me a little work to get out of the hatch and not bend it. Someone's gonna need to keep those spider things busy while I'm bein' a contortionist." He squeezed her shoulder. "You can do it. That's why you got the blue oval on your costume. It means somethin'."

Maia's mouth went dry, and she licked her lips with a tongue that felt like sandpaper. The whining of the spiders' drills continued. She needed to make herself *move.* She could almost hear Sara berating her, telling her to move her ass.

She didn't have to climb the ladder to reach the hatch. She reached up with her free hand and pulled on the lever to break the seal. Icy air leaked around the edges of the hatch. The drilling sounds stopped immediately.

They'd heard the hatch unseal.

"Go," Burleigh said.

Maia went.

One deep breath and she flung open the hatch. She eschewed the ladder and flexed her muscular legs instead. It was like she was diving into the sea, with her hands over her head and the boat hook resting along the back of her shoulder. Instead, she jumped through the hatch to land on the lifeboat's upper hull hard enough to dent it under one foot.

A quick glance around told her there were seven or eight of the weird mechanical creatures crouched in various spots along the lifeboat's hull. They were frozen in place as if staring at her in shock, even though they had no features that could conceivably be described as eyes or even gaping mouths. Despite the twilight darkness from the storm, they seemed to glow with some kind of internal light, for she could see them clearly despite the blowing sleet. Lightning flashed and thunder boomed overhead and the spiders must have taken it as a signal, for they closed with her.

Maia shrieked and leaped from the top of the lifeboat, not even pausing to consider whether Harry's ice dome could support her weight. She slid and bounced down the slope to reach the slushy ice field upon which they had come to rest. She spun around, boat hook at the ready, and saw four of the spiders scuttling after her. Their legs ended in sharp points that dug into the ice like pickaxes.

Burleigh wrestled himself through the top hatch and yelled as more spiders converged upon him. "What the shit . . . *Get off of me!*" He brought his axe down upon the mass of metallic creatures and they splashed apart like he'd split a paint can.

Maia screamed and swung the boat hook in an awkward down-sweeping arc. She caught a spider with the hooked head and sent it flying toward the roiling ocean like she was driving a golf ball down the fairway.

Burleigh crashed down to the ice beside her. He kicked another spider and it flew away as well. "You okay, kid?"

"Yeah." Maia poked the business end of her boat hook at another spider, shoving it back several yards before it resumed its scuttle toward her. She jabbed and swung at them, doing her best to keep them away from her.

Lightning flashed again and she caught more motion out of the corner of her eye. When she turned to look, her knees felt like they were about to buckle.

A much bigger spider the size of a large dog approached down the side of the ice dome, moving with grim determination on five legs the size of signposts. It drove one foot downward and broke through the dome, falling off balance for a moment before it pulled its leg free.

"Where d-did that come from?" Maia cried.

"I got it. You keep the small ones off me." Burleigh raised his axe. "Come on, you gruesome motherfucker. I got a lifetime of anger issues to work out."

Moving with eerie silence, the spider reached the ground and stomped toward Burleigh and Maia.

Burleigh roared his challenge and brought his axe down upon the body of the creature, striking it dead on center mass. The axe split it right in half and the two halves collapsed in on themselves like he'd cut through the middle of a table.

A spider crawled onto Maia's foot and she shrieked. Burleigh's massive strike had distracted her from her task. She kicked but the spider gripped her with mechanical determination. She jabbed at it with the boat hook, trying to dislodge it, but its legs had somehow laced themselves around her foot until it felt more like a metallic slipper than a spider. She'd spear her own foot if she tried to really hit it.

"Burleigh, it's *sticky*," she screamed, not having the proper vocabulary to describe what had happened.

"Agh!" he yelled, and Maia's eyes widened as she saw what had happened with the giant spider.

It hadn't sensibly stayed down in pieces after Burleigh cut it apart. Instead, it flowed like honey, stretching into long, thin metallic tendrils that swung themselves around him. He looked like he was fighting a giant mass of salt-water taffy instead of a discrete creature. The strands were wrapping around his legs and arms, binding them so he couldn't use his strength.

"Help!" Maia screamed.

A blur of motion, Tanya emerged from the top of the lifeboat, wielding both of the boat's hatchets in each hand. She raced around Burleigh, hacking and chopping at the strands imprisoning him, substituting pure speed for precision. Despite the treacherous surface, slick with slush and fresh ice, she seemed more sure-footed than ever as she fought to free her comrades.

Another spider crawled onto Maia and merged with the one already encapsulating her foot. She got the boat hook wedged between them and tried to lever them apart until the haft broke. Left with a splintered handle, she speared it down to impale another approaching spider to the ice. It wiggled its legs, trying to move past the stick holding it fast. It started to split itself apart when the ice around it opened up and swallowed it whole.

Harry stood atop the lifeboat with Cale supporting him as he directed the ice like Moses parting the Red

Sea. Waves of ice, as fluid as the ocean that had tossed them like so much debris, swamped the roving spiders, crushing them beneath its weight and preventing them from moving.

A sneaky spider that should have been out of range lengthened a leg and tripped up Tanya. She fell and a dozen more spiders swarmed onto her. Maia screamed as she realized more of them skittered out of the darkness. A wave of gleaming metal, all legs and eerie silence, overran the top of the lifeboat, swamping Cale and Harry beneath it. Metal stuck Maia's legs together and she toppled. The wave swallowed her as well, wrapping her up tight in a metallic tomb like she'd been locked inside an iron maiden.

Chapter Eleven

From Maia's playlist: "Flaming Telepaths" - Blue Öyster Cult

A swaying, lurching motion told Maia that she was being carried by the strangely fluid metal encasing her. At first, she'd held her breath, afraid she would discover no air was available and strangle. Then it occurred to her that if the spider things had wanted her dead, they wouldn't have wrapped her up and carried her off somewhere. They could have killed her easily enough by pouring themselves into her lungs and tearing her apart from the inside. She took a tentative breath. Air passed into her lungs, albeit with a peculiar, chemical flavor. She tried to move but found she could not. However the metal had wrapped itself around her had effectively immobilized her in such a way that her parahuman strength had no effect. She tried calling out to the others but heard nothing but the tinny sound of her own voice, reflected against the metal only a fraction of an inch from her mouth and nose.

The claustrophobia was terrifying. Her heart raced and panic scrabbled at her the way the spiders had come racing toward her. Spiders! Whether they had eight legs or five, why did it have to be spiders? What did they want? Or did they want anything? She didn't think they were alive—at least, not the way she was. They behaved like machines, following a program with limited imagination to fulfill its parameters. She knew there were a few parahumans in the world whose bodies were made of metal, like Detroit Steel and

Nickel, and even those who could control metal and make it move and flow, the way the Hero Academy principal MetalBlade did. Even if there was a parahuman who could make spider machines like those she and her team had fought, the big question was why.

Just Cause Arctic Circle didn't have much in the way of front line fighters, and that was a strategic decision by the higher-ups in the Parahuman Resources Administration. The need for fighting parahumans would be reduced in a region without much in the way of choice targets. The team had been optimized as rescuers, an international Coast Guard for the Arctic Circle. The worst thing they were likely to face was, in all honesty, the storm that had just bested them. Supervillains were pretty far down the list of likely possibilities.

So who or what had set these spiders upon the team, and why? Then she remembered the first one had been on the *Atlanta Nights*. Maybe they had been transporting the spider things and one had gotten out. Or all of them. Had the crew been wrapped up in metal the way she had and carried off to . . . wherever it was they were going? Or perhaps the spider had come on board from somewhere else.

Maia had so many questions, and no answers, and she was still being carried along in her cocoon. She didn't know what else to do, so she tried to sleep. At least it would help her conserve her energy for when she might need it. With her eyes shut, she could almost imagine the metal wrapped around her limbs was a blanket or that she was underwater. The swaying motion of what seemed to be overland travel could have been soothing, like the rocking of a train or bus . . . if she hadn't been a prisoner.

The one thing she knew, that kept her from full-on panic, was that she wasn't alone. She'd seen the others wrapped up by the liquid metal spiders. They all had to be going to the same place. At least, she hoped they were. If the others were just . . . gone, she didn't know what she would do.

* * *

The cessation of the swaying movement awakened Maia with a start, and for what seemed like an eternity, there was nothing but the sound of her blood rushing in her ears, the whisper of her breathing, and the gentle thumping of her heartbeat beneath it all. Had they reached their final destination or had they stopped for some other reason?

Metal poured away from her face and around her body like it was flowing into a drain, leaving her lying on a cold, rocky surface. At first she was completely blind in the darkness, but as her eyes adjusted, she became aware of shapes, highlighted by faint luminescence with no discernible source. The air felt different than it had on the ice floe. It was warmer, drier, and had a distinct metallic tang to it. She wondered if that was a byproduct of the metal spider things. Maybe they were alive in some way after all, and they had brought her to their nest.

Her surroundings grew brighter at a slow but steady rate, like someone turning a dial. She was in a rough-hewn or natural cave of some sort. It was hard to tell if it was natural or if someone had dug it out—she was no expert in spelunking. She'd always thought caves were full of mushrooms and bats and blind fish. This one was full of something else.

The source of the illumination became apparent as faint traceries of minerals brightened, giving the walls around her the appearance of a static image of bluish-white lightning. The glowing veins spread across the uneven floor, walls, and ceiling as well. The room was roughly pentagonal, and the walls didn't stick up at ninety degrees as might be expected. Instead, more pentagonal shapes came up at oblique angles, meeting again at another pentagonal face upon the ceiling. Something about the shape seemed strangely familiar to her, and then she remembered gaming at the Hero Academy.

There was a regular Saturday afternoon gaming group at the Hero Academy. It had been going on, as far as Maia knew, for as many years as the Academy had been in existence. She'd gone to a few of them but never really got the hang of role-playing games. She suspected that might have been due to her extremely sheltered upbringing. She didn't have a whole lot of imagination, and she knew it. When presented with the infinite theoretical possibilities of role-playing games, she tended to freeze with indecision, and no amount of coaching from her classmates and fellow players had managed to break her of that habit. At last, she'd settled for attending occasionally, the way one might go see a movie once in a while, to enjoy the story and the camaraderie without being required to participate.

Most of the games involved dice of varying shapes and faces, and she was pretty sure she was inside a twelve-sided die.

There was a metallic panel on one face, which might have been a door or a hatch, but without a handle or hinges that she could see. Her captors, either the controllers of the spiders or the spiders themselves, were nowhere to be seen. She was lying on the floor of the room, and the uneven rocks jabbed her in the back of her head, so she sat up to get a better sense of what was around her. The room had no furnishings, no decorations beyond the glowing minerals in the walls.

"H-hello?" Her mouth was dry and she felt dehydrated, as if the air was sucking all the moisture from her body. She licked her lips with a dry tongue and tried to generate a little spit. "Hello?" she called. No reply came immediately and she wondered how far she was from her teammates, or if they were even in the same place. She suspected they probably were, because they'd all been captured at the same time.

She went over to the wall panel holding the door and touched it gingerly, half expecting some kind of horrible response like a shock or an alarm, but nothing happened. The metal was cool but not icy cold, telling her she wasn't in some sort of room right at the surface of the Arctic. How long had she been asleep, carried by the flowing metal spiders? How fast had they gone? So many questions plagued her, but no answers presented themselves. She tried to push it open, but there were no visible hinges. There was no way for her to pull on it, or to get a grip to lift it. She steeled herself and drove her fist into it, hoping she wouldn't hurt herself. The door rang like a bass drum but she didn't so much as dent it.

What she did notice, however, was a small bit of sand shook loose from the rock at the edge of the panel. She leaned in to look more closely and rubbed her thumb along the edge. It felt crumbly, like sandstone. She wondered how solid it really was. When she pulled her hand back, a few grains clung to the skin of her thumb. She knew it was an important clue, and wished she had someone to ask about it. Without her teammates nearby, she was going to have to depend upon only herself to get out of her predicament. "Come on, Devilfish," she said aloud. "This is a gamer puzzle. There's got to be a way out. There's always a way out."

She hoped she was right about that. In games, there was always some way for the players to advance, but this wasn't a game, and maybe her captors hadn't thought to make a secret panel or hidden counterweight or something to allow her to escape the supposedly inescapable room.

Time for personal inventory, she thought, and took stock of what she still possessed. For starters, she still had her full costume, including her goggles and face mask with its extra lungful of compressed air. Her belly pouch was still strapped around her shoulders. In it she found a trove of tools that might make her escape possible. She had two twenty-ounce water bottles, both full. Two food bars Tanya had given her and a chocolate bar she'd forgotten she'd stashed. She wouldn't starve and wouldn't go thirsty, at least not immediately. Her radio didn't appear to have survived the fight, for it was in pieces. She suspected it wouldn't have done her any good anyway if she was underground.

Then she found the thing that made her crow aloud with delight: a stainless steel multitool. It had been at the very bottom of her pack, and she remembered she'd thrown it in there back at headquarters. There was room for a lot more in her pack, but besides the tool the only thing remaining was the curled-up dead metal leg of the spider. She put everything but the multitool back into her pack after taking a sip of water to moisten her parched mouth. Whomever had imprisoned her hadn't bothered to search her, which was, perhaps, strangest of all.

She made a thorough search of the room, checking floor, wall panels, and ceiling twice over to make sure she didn't miss anything. The luminescent mineral lines were softer than the surrounding rock, which she discovered with the multitool blade. She wasn't sure they were mineral upon closer investigation. Maybe they were more like a fiber optic plastic. She thought about seeing if she could cut into one, or pry it loose from the surrounding rock, but put that aside for the moment. Doing damage merely for the sake of doing damage wasn't her style, and if it didn't seem like it would be likely to assist in her getting out, it was wasted energy.

She returned her energy to the door. It was the only apparent way in or out of the room, without so much as a ventilation duct to provide her with air. That thought made her heart race. What if she was running out of air? But then she set it aside. She'd been able to breathe even with the fluid metal surrounding her. Whatever else the spiders had intended, they had kept her alive. She had to assume they did the same for her teammates.

Spiders. They were such an odd design, with five limbs instead of eight and no apparent internal workings. Why would anything have such an unusual number of legs? Maybe they were more like starfish than spiders. Combined with their ability to flow and recombine, she was reminded of the nanotech sludge that formed the basis of the Just Cause Combat Simulation Chamber, which she and the rest of the

Hero Academy students got to train in a few times a year. It was a masterpiece of engineering. Millions of microscopic robots used storage vats full of raw materials to create simulated locations where the heroes could cut loose and use their powers. It was faster than using teams of construction workers to build training sets out of actual materials, after which everything would have to be torn down and much of it thrown away. The initial expense had been costly but once the CSC had been designed and built, it became a standard for all Just Cause facilities. The teams could then train in a variety of environments—urban and suburban, indoor and outdoor, city and wilderness. It would help them prepare for any eventuality the strategists could imagine.

Well, except for Arctic Circle, Maia thought with a wry smile. What were they going to do, simulate shipwrecks and ice floes and fighting off robotic spider things?

The way the spiders moved and shaped themselves reminded mind of the nanotech of the CSC, and she wondered if they might be colonies of nanites after all. That would explain much about their behavior. From what she knew, nanites didn't have enough ability to store or process information themselves, so they had to be controlled and directed from a central facility. That meant someone was in charge, and had for whatever reason decided to go capture themselves a superhero team.

Maia didn't know if she was right or wrong in her assessment, but she knew one thing. Whomever had done it was going to pay for their crimes. She would see to that. Sara's death would be unavenged. Old Testament-style.

Using the file from her multitool, she attacked the rock around the edge of the door. Seams were always the weakest parts of any creation and she thought perhaps she could loosen the entire door in its surrounding parent material. She wasn't disappointed. The rock appeared solid enough at first glance, but as she poked and scraped at it, bits of gravel and sand came loose, like the rock had been compressed into place like cement. She hacked and chopped and made slow but steady progress through the material. She didn't know where she was going, but as Burleigh had said, she was making great time.

Chapter Twelve

From Maia's playlist: "Hall of the Mountain King" - <u>Rainbow</u>

Rotten rock crumbled away under Maia's relentless onslaught. She had no way to keep track of the time she spent digging away at it, but she fell into a rhythm, digging at the same pace as the songs in her head. She replayed song after classic rock song, singing along with them under her breath. She chopped the multitool at the rock with every downbeat, and wished she had her phone so she could really listen to the songs in her mind.

Then in the middle of a tune by Boston, the tip of the tool burst through the other side of the door and she was so startled by the sudden lack of resistance she nearly lost it through the hole. She pulled it back so it was safely on her side of the door, her heart pounding at how close she'd come to failing in her escape attempt. A gentle current passed through the hole she'd opened, carrying with it a faint hint of sea salt.

She bent to peer through the hole. It was small and she couldn't see any details about what lay beyond it. She couldn't hear anything through it either—not even the sound of ventilation, which most people didn't notice at all unless it shut off. Although she could smell the sea, she couldn't hear it, nor the sound of the hurricane and its attendant thundering. She was probably deep enough underground to be below the permafrost, or else the caves were warmed artificially. She hadn't felt heat radiating from anything in her cell, but that didn't mean there wasn't some sort of warm-air exchange going on.

One spring break, she and some of her classmates had toured a publicly accessible cave south of Denver, called Cave of the Winds. There was a sign posted there stating the cave was the same temperature year-round, no matter the weather on the surface. She knew the deeper one went, the warmer it got. Her classmate Lindsay was the daughter of a prison guard at Deep Six. Lindsay had said how important the air conditioning was at the underground prison because without it, it was hot enough to put inmates and guards in real distress. Maia wasn't roasting, so she probably wasn't as far underground as Deep Six. That didn't tell her a whole lot, but it was a starting point.

The hole she'd made was another starting point, and since nobody had come to investigate, she figured she might as well keep going.

She used the multitool to chip away more of the rotten rock, working as quickly as she dared to widen it without breaking the tool. If it shattered, that would make escape far more difficult. Still, nobody was hassling her about the noise and mess she was making. It was like her captors didn't even care. After they'd spent so much effort to grab her and the others, how were they not watching her like hawks? Spider hawks. Robot spider hawks. If anyone came to stop her, she decided, she'd fight them until she couldn't move. It didn't matter that she wasn't particularly good at it. She was a graduate of the Hero Academy, and part of Just Cause, and she wasn't going to be anybody's prisoner.

She got the hole widened enough to stick her arm through. She tucked the multitool safely into her pack, and pressed herself against the door, feeling through the hole in the wall to see if she could find a handle or switch or something to release herself. At the side of the door, her hand encountered a flat metal plate with a hole in its center, like the mouth of a pencil sharpener. That made her think of the spiders and their legs. She went back into her pack and found the curled up severed leg. It couldn't be *that* easy, could it?

Maia uncurled the leg until it was more or less straight, then stretched her arm back through the hole she'd made. She was careful to keep a solid hold on the leg while maneuvering it to the right angle. If it could be a key, and she let it slip from her fingers, she would have to dig through a lot more rock before she could reach it. She was certain *someone* would come stop her if she continued for much longer.

The tip of the severed leg found the hole and she fed it inside. The click of the lock releasing was almost anticlimactic. The door swung upward from a hinge on its topmost point. Maia pulled her arm back through the hole and put the leg back in her pouch so she wouldn't lose it. She went through the door before anyone noticed it was open and closed it remotely, assuming that was a thing that could happen. She was loose inside the prison, and she had a key.

The cell door had opened into a passageway with a pentagonal cross section, approximately the same diameter of the room she'd just escaped. Other doors were set along the lower face of the wall to one side, while the strange luminescent mineral veins ran along the other four faces of the corridor. The corridor itself dead-ended after two doors to Maia's left. She went to the last door and used the spider leg to open it.

Tanya was sitting inside against the far wall and leaped to her feet when the door swung open. "Maia! What are you doing? How did you get out?"

Maia held up the spider leg. "I have a key."

"*Bozhe moi.* That is brilliant."

"The spider things didn't take away any of my gear. I had a multitool and used it to chip away the rock beside my door. It crumbled pretty easily. I'm thinking that maybe it's kind of old, yeah?"

"I do not know. I am not a geologist." Tanya stepped out into the corridor. She squeezed Maia with a brief hug. "I am glad to see you."

"I'm glad to see you," Maia said. "Did they leave you with your equipment too?"

"Yes, but I had nothing to dig into the rock with. I do not carry much, because weight matters for speedsters. I have a ration bar, a pouch of water, but on the bright side, I have lost my stupid antlers." She laughed. "I also have my radio, but it is broken."

"Mine's broken too. I don't know if they'd be any good here, yeah?"

"Why do you think they allowed us to retain our gear? Prisoners should be stripped and searched to prevent exactly what you have done."

Maia shrugged. "I don't know. Maybe we can ask them when we find them. Let's check these other doors and see who else is here, yeah?"

"Yeah."

The next door revealed Harry, whose pale complexion and general weakness suggested he was suffering the aftereffects of the adrenaline injection he'd received during the combat. He had dark circles under his eyes and his hands shook. "Boy, am I glad to see the two of you," he said. "I feel terrible."

"You look terrible as well," Tanya said.

"Thanks for the second opinion." Harry managed a weak smile.

Maia gave him one of her water bottles. "Here, I hope this helps."

He took a grateful sip. "Thank you."

"What is this place?" Tanya asked.

"No idea," Harry said. "But it's weird."

"Is very weird," Tanya said.

"Why do you think it's weird?" Maia asked. "I mean, besides them letting me dig myself to freedom with the gear they left me."

"I've been thinking. What else could I do? After that shot Michelle gave me, I don't have enough strength to do anything else. I'm pretty sure I slept all the way here, wherever *here* is."

"Underground, still near the ocean, yeah?" Maia said.

Harry looked at her and nodded. "I think you're probably right. So those spider things are weird.

They've got five legs instead of eight, which is unnatural as hell. But then this place we're in uses both five and six as fundamental base numbers. Pentagonal and dodecahedral walls."

"I do not know this word," Tanya said.

"It means twelve-sided. I assume your cell looked like mine and it was made of interlocking pentagons. Humans don't do that unless they're making geodesic domes. Humans like right angles. Insects use hexagons. Maybe these things use pentagons the same way."

Maia blinked. "You think this is a . . . a bug nest?"

Harry shrugged. "No. I don't know what it is. Whoever made it approaches construction very differently than most people. Come on, let's find the others."

They went down the corridor, opening doors to release the remainder of their teammates. The next three cells contained Cale, Burleigh, and Michelle, who grimaced in pain at the slightest movement.

"How are you feeling?" Cale asked her.

"Like an elephant sat on my chest. No offense." Michelle nodded toward Maia. "An elephant who saved my life." She coughed.

Maia wasn't sure if that was any better, but she'd take the compliment for what it was.

None of her teammates had been searched or had their gear taken either. The spiders had even left Burleigh his axe, and he'd put it to good use in his own cell. He'd managed to hack away a good amount of rock from around his own door, but hadn't progressed enough to make a hole big enough for him to squeeze through. "The rock is firmer further away from the door. I'm not sure I could have gotten out before dying from thirst or hunger." He looked around. "You don't suppose there's a mess hall around here somewhere, do you?"

"How can you think of food at time like this?" Tanya asked him.

Burleigh smiled. "I'm hungry."

Maia handed him one of her food bars and he nodded in gratitude.

Cale pointed to the remaining six doors in the corridor. "We need to check all these rooms to make sure nobody else is being held here. The way the crew of the *Atlanta Nights* simply disappeared makes me wonder if they might be here. It can't be a coincidence that we found one of the spider things on board."

Maia proceeded to open each door in the corridor but the remaining cells were empty.

"Pretty clever how you figured that out with the spider leg," Burleigh said. "Don't lose that thing."

"Why do you think it died when Burleigh hit it instead of just turning into liquid and reforming the way the others did?" Cale asked.

"Nanotech," Michelle said. She had an arm over Tanya's shoulders for support.

Harry pointed at her. "Right. I was thinking that it reminds me of CSC tech."

Cale rubbed his jaw. "Destroyer used nanotech. I wonder if he was involved in this place somehow."

Maia knew who Destroyer was, thanks to her History of Parahumans course at the Academy. He'd been a supervillain and a sworn enemy of Just Cause for almost four decades before he died helping the very same team defend the Earth against the Hind invasion. There was even a statue of him in the Memorial Garden in Just Cause Denver, along with many other heroes who'd given their lives in the line of duty.

"What would he have been doing in the Arctic?" Harry asked. "There's nothing up here."

"It doesn't have to have been him," Burleigh said. "There must be other people working with nanotech. He didn't invent it."

"Nanotech has a lot of fluidic potential," Harry said. "Like in that old Terminator movie. Liquid metal. That could explain the construction of the spider things when they don't have any differentiation in their construction."

"So what about this, yeah?" Maia held up the leg.

"Maybe when the lumberjack here hit it, he disrupted it severely enough that the individual nanites weren't able to reconfigure themselves. Like if you interrupt a computer when it's updating itself, it sometimes screws it up beyond all repair." Harry shrugged. "I'm not really an engineer."

"It's as good a working theory as anything else we have," Cale said. "I think we need to get moving, though. They might have let us get out of our cells, but I can't imagine they're going to let us wander through their base or whatever this is without stopping us."

Burleigh slapped his axe into his palm. The sharp snap echoed off the walls around them. "We're right behind you, Fearless Leader."

Cale didn't look particularly thrilled at the notion, but like it or not, he was in charge, and the rest of the team was looking to him now Sara was gone. "Harry, you're promoted. If I do anything you think is really stupid, let me know."

Harry raised his hand.

Cale sighed. "Yes?"

"I think Burleigh's a better choice than me."

"Why's that?" Cale asked.

"Yeah, how come you don't want the job?" Burleigh grinned. "What do you know that I don't?"

"I know that you're a better leader than you think you are, and we tend to listen to you. Also, it's easier for me to focus on being team medic if I don't also have to plan and strategize and stuff. Also, I'm shit at giving orders."

Burleigh shrugged. "I'd've followed them."

Tanya and Michelle both made faces, suggesting that neither of them particularly liked the idea of Harry making decisions that involved anything serious.

Cale nodded. "Harry, good point. Are you going to take it personally if I change my mind?"

"God, no. Please and thank you and all those other Canadian things."

Chapter Thirteen

From Maia's playlist: "All Cats Are Grey" - <u>The Cure</u>

The team advanced up the corridor, full of caution and expecting trouble. Like the other construction or excavation they had encountered, the corridor didn't turn at right angles. Instead, it turned at angles Harry said were seventy-two degrees with no branches. Maia wasn't sure how far the corridor went, but she thought it was an unusually long distance. She asked Burleigh about it. "Why keep the prisoners so far away from everything else?"

"We don't know that we were far away from everything else. The walls could have been full of all the important stuff and we just walked right by it."

"Do you think this is the way out?"

"If it's not, I don't know where else to suggest."

The corridor took another turn and they paused, for instead of turning left or right, it took a steep seventy-two-degree drop down. If they'd been moving in complete darkness, they might have gone right over the edge, not realizing it until it was too late.

"I'm going to see how far down it goes," Cale said. "This will be really difficult to get back up if we need to." He went over the edge, his own illumination making a ring of light against the tunnel walls.

Michelle peeked over the edge. "I don't know how I'll get down if that's our only choice."

"Getting down is easy," Harry said. "The trick is not to die while doing it."

"Thanks for that," Michelle said. "Nice to know you're on my side."

Cale flew back up a minute later. "It's about sixty feet down and ends on another horizontal surface. There's no graduation between the angles, either. If you slide down, you're going to hit the bottom pretty hard."

"Why would they put sharp drop like this here?" Tanya asked.

"Maybe the spiders can climb it without any trouble, yeah?" Maia suggested. "Or it's to keep us from wandering too far."

Burleigh kicked at the floor, then tapped the haft of his axe against it. Rock splintered and cracked, suggesting portions of it were as rotten as the rock around their doors. "I think I can cut steps into this. They won't be perfect, but it'll help keep us all from dying."

An idea came to Maia. "Let me go down ahead of you," she said. "If somebody slips and falls, I can catch them, yeah?"

Burleigh glanced at Cale, who nodded. "That's a good idea," said the Canadian. "Take Burleigh's axe down with you. Use it as a brake. I'll bring it back up the slope to him."

"Now hold on a minute," Burleigh began, but Maia had her hands out to him already. He sighed and placed the axe in her grip. "This is my baby," he said. "Be nice to her."

Maia hefted the heavy weapon. "I'll take good care of her, I promise." She looked at Cale. "What's at the bottom?"

"More corridor."

"Light my way down?"

"Of course. Burleigh, mind the store."

"Okay, but hurry. It's almost time for my smoke break."

Maia considered whether to use the bladed or hooked end of axe head as the brake and decided the hook was probably going to work better. She slipped her hand through the heavy leather strap at the end of the handle and squeezed it tight as she inched herself over the edge. Sixty feet, she told herself. That wasn't too far. It was four or five stories, sure, but she was strong and tough and she could survive that fall even without slowing herself . . . at least, that's what she thought as she passed the point of no return and slid down the slope. She squeaked in fear and slammed the axe into the rock. The hook bit, tore through rotten rock, then bit again. Every time it caught, pieces of rock would rip loose until she was descending amid a shower of stones, gravel, and dust. She almost hit the bottom before she was ready, but she'd struck her final blow at just the right time and reached the floor no harder than if she'd jumped off a second-floor balcony onto soft lawn. She tucked and rolled, the way she'd been taught at the Academy, and wound up back on her feet in a corridor nearly identical to the one at the top of the slope. The crashing of rock and gravel echoed up and down the hall.

"Maia, are you all right?" Cale sounded equally concerned and astonished as he hovered above her.

"Yeah," she said. "The ground broke my fall." She handed him Burleigh's axe.

Cale snorted. "I'll go help the others. Watch and listen." He flew back up the slope.

Maia kept her eyes and ears wide open. The dimly lit corridor didn't reveal any new arrivals—spider-like or otherwise. She couldn't believe nobody had come to investigate the racket she had made in her descent or the regular chopping sounds as Burleigh cut steps into the rocks for the others.

Soon, she could see Burleigh on approach, hunching down and swinging his axe as the others followed behind. Harry helped Michelle the best he could but as they reached the bottom it became clear that she was in great pain. "Does anybody have any medical supplies left?" Cale asked.

Nobody did.

Michelle grimaced. "I don't know how much more walking I can do. It really hurts to move and to breathe."

"I know, and I'm sorry," Cale said. "Burleigh, can you carry her?"

"Of course. All aboard the Lumberjack Express." Burleigh handed his axe to Maia, apparently having decided she was trustworthy enough to look after it for him.

They advanced down the new corridor, Cale and Maia taking the lead, followed by Tanya and Harry, with Burleigh carrying Michelle at the rear. The corridor went on for a long way without turns or branches. Irregular sections of the luminescent veins in the walls were dark, like damaged neon tubes. They found a section where part of the wall had collapsed—likely due to more of the rotten rock—and Harry used Maia's multitool to pry loose a piece of the unlit luminescent material.

"It's some kind of fiber optics," he said as he turned it around underneath Cale's brilliance. "Look at this. It's like glass or plastic, not hollow." He looked at the damaged wall. "This stuff isn't natural. It was made and put here."

"It looks like it was grown here," Maia said. "Right through the walls, yeah? There aren't any seams."

"Lends more credence to the nanotech theory," Harry said.

The team continued onward down the bland, featureless corridor. It went on straight for hundreds or maybe thousands of feet without turning, climbing, or dropping again. "This is crazy, yeah?" Maia said. "Who would build something like this? Why would they put the cells so far away from . . . from . . ."

"Everything," Burleigh finished her sentence. "And there's no guards or anythin'. This whole place feels like it isn't complete. Like it's still under construction."

"None of the architecture makes sense," Harry said. "Especially in the Arctic. I wonder if this is some kind of relic installation left over from the Cold War."

"All Arctic wars would be cold," Burleigh said.

"You know what I mean," Harry said.

"You're talking about the DEW Line," Cale said. "My grandfather worked on building those."

"What is DEW Line?" Tanya asked.

"Distant Early Warning Line. It was to detect any bombers or missiles being launched from the Soviet Union," Cale said. "It was a good theory, but didn't work so well in practice. The whole thing was shut down thirty or forty years ago."

"My grandfather also worked on early warning installations," Tanya said. "In Siberia. He was not given a choice."

"Well, it was a different time then," Cale said, doing his Canadian best to make peace before tensions rose. Things were tense enough with the team exhausted, lost, and dismayed after losing one of their own.

"Hey, I think the corridor's opening up." Maia squinted at a dark pentagonal shadow that suggested the corridor's end in a larger space of some kind.

Cale directed his light further down the corridor. "I think you're right, Maia. Tanya, with me, please."

"*Da.*" Tanya trotted down the corridor with Cale above her, illuminating the path.

Burleigh sat down right where he was, carefully keeping Michelle in his lap like he was cuddling a sleeping child. Maia realized the metaphor was apt, for Michelle's eyes were shut and her breathing was shallow but regular. "Is she okay?" She kept her voice soft.

"I think so," Burleigh said. "She's hurtin', so it's good that she's out."

"I feel so bad about breaking her ribs." Maia hung her head. "I mean, I know I saved her life, but I hate that I hurt her doing it, yeah?"

"You did a good thing," Burleigh said. "Don't ever apologize for saving a life. That's what we do."

"They're coming back," Harry said. "They don't look happy."

In fact, Maia thought Tanya looked pale and afraid. Cale had pulled his hood and mask back to uncover his face again, and he looked sick to his stomach. "What is it?" Maia asked.

Tanya said softly, "Is bad."

Chapter Fourteen

From Maia's playlist: "We Are the Dead" - <u>David Bowie</u>

The corridor opened into a large chamber. Maia couldn't tell how large for sure, because the luminescent material didn't spread out across the chamber walls. Instead, it coalesced along a central path. The sound of their footsteps echoed enough that she thought it was probably quite large, like the interior of an airplane hangar. The air was still, like the calm before a storm.

The central path had pedestals of varying sizes flanking it. The glowing tendrils threaded up the sides of each pedestal to faintly illuminate it. Atop each pedestal was a clear jar or tank, filled with a transparent fluid and *something* inside each one. Dead creatures—she assumed they were dead, because the alternative was much worse—floated in the tanks, suspended in the fluid without touching the sides of the tanks. Some of them looked like creatures she had seen before, crabs and lobsters and fish, but others were strange and disturbing, more like creatures from a nightmare, with armor plating and tentacles and even some with scales and claws. All of them had something in common: they looked like another creature had been merged with them and was trying to tear its way out of the host animals' body. It wasn't like they were parasites, growing inside the animal and ripping or eating themselves free. It was more like one animal was growing out of the other, like a new appendage or a cancer.

Even with the animals that weren't particularly pretty to begin with, it was horrible. Their bodies were twisted in death with teeth bared—for those that had them—in pain. Oddly jointed limbs, wrapped in dull, chitinous material, grew from torsos and abdomens, ending in sharp claws. In some cases, the limbs curled back inward to embed those claws in the host creature's body, as if it were trying to cut itself apart. Maia felt her stomach turn as she regarded an Arctic fox with its head split open by a growth that resembled a five-petaled flower, albeit with teeth like a shark's on the inside of each petal.

Tanya spat into the darkness twice, keeping her gaze toward the floor so she wouldn't see any more of the horrors in the tanks. Maia knew how she felt but, like witnessing a car crash, she couldn't make herself look away from the monstrous mutations.

"What in the name of God . . ." Harry whispered.

"Ain't no God here," Burleigh said. "Only death."

Cale's glow lit a larger tank, which held sea creature with a long neck and tail, and flappers instead of feet. A single jointed leg grew at a crazy angle from the base of its spine.

"That looks like a dinosaur, yeah?" Maia's voice sounded tiny and pathetic in the cavernous chamber.

"That's impossible," Cale said. "It's some kind of . . . mutated alligator or something."

"In the Arctic?" Harry asked. "Unlikely."

"And it's more likely that it's a dinosaur?" Cale snorted in doubt, but he didn't look away from the creature in question for several long seconds before turning to continue along the path.

"Maybe it's like the Loch Ness Monster." Maia suggested. "That's like a dinosaur or something, yeah?"

"No, it's . . ." Cale stopped, for his light had illuminated the next tank, which contained something that nobody could have described as anything other than a saber-toothed tiger with a tawny coat devoid of any stripes or spots. It appeared to have died in throes of agony. Half its head had sprouted the petal-like mouth that had grown from the Arctic fox's body further back. Three long, jointed legs grew from the same side of its body as the toothy petals, and deep gashes in its side showed a shiny carapace-like material beneath the fur.

"God, it's horrible," Michelle said. "Who would do this to all these creatures?"

"It's definitely some weird-ass *Island of Dr. Moreau* shit here, that's for sure," Burleigh said.

Harry grimaced as he stepped closer to the saber-tooth to take a better look. "All these animals have the same kind of growths. It's like they were transforming into another creature and died in the process. Some kind of giant insect."

"That's the legs, yeah?" Maia asked.

"I don't know what else to call it. I've never heard of anything like this. It's some kind of chimera, but it's crossing species barriers. That's impossible." Harry shook his head. " Sure, we're all parahumans here, and impossible according to most laws of physics. But this is something else. Something darker."

"It's cruel," Michelle said, coughing. "All these animals look like they were in pain when they died."

"We're forgettin' somethin' even more important," Burleigh said. "I know Cale said that wasn't a dinosaur back there, but this is a goddamn saber-tooth tiger. Anyone want to argue that with me?"

Nobody spoke.

"Look, I'm no scientist, but even I know that saber-tooths are extinct and have been for thousands of years. And if that's really a dinosaur back there . . . how long has this place been here?"

Silence settled upon the team like a cloak as they considered the implications of Burleigh's words. "If it's true . . ." Harry said. "It predates humanity. By a lot."

Maia looked around. "Where's Tanya?" She raised her voice. "Tanya?"

"Tanya, where are you?" Burleigh called.

The Russian speedster was nowhere to be seen. Cale rose in the air and brightened his glow, trying to illuminate enough of the chamber that they might be able to see where she had gone. "Tanya, sound off!" More and more of the tanks became visible as his light chased away the darkness until the team could see what they'd thought of as a chamber was more like the inside of a domed football stadium. Some truly gargantuan tanks were placed further away, containing more dinosaur-like creatures and some giant cetaceans, including a beluga whale with its skull split apart by a giant version of the petal-mouth thing. Maia wanted to close her eyes, but knew she could never unsee the things like a squid trying to tear itself apart with its own tentacles.

Tanya was a couple dozen yards away from the rest of the team, standing frozen in front of a tank with a shadowy figure inside. Cale flew to her and the rest of the team hurried along the ground, trying not to look too closely at any more of the ruined and tormented corpses within their tanks.

"Oh no . . ." Maia saw what was in the tank and turned away, unable to look.

Burleigh put an arm around her. "It's okay, kid. You don't have to look."

The tank held a human or proto-human female. She was nude, with thick, dark body hair on her legs, arms, and head. She had a broad face with a jaw jutting forward and a heavy brow ridge. The familiar toothed petals had emerged from her throat and five small but well-formed legs grew from her torso, two under each of her arms and one emerging from her abdomen. Her legs looked withered, as if they were rotting away. Her arms were disfigured, with chitin showing through splits in the skin and claws emerging from the backs of her wrists.

"They did it to a person," Tanya said softly. "They took her and did this to her and then watched her die like others before sticking her in a tank. This place . . . this is hell."

"I don't believe in hell," Cale said. "But this is a terrible place, and we need to find our way out so we don't wind up in these tanks ourselves. We don't need to keep checking out the scenery any longer. We need to find the exit. I don't know why nobody seems to be looking for us after our escape, but they could start at any time."

"They could be looking for us now," Harry said. "Maybe they just haven't caught up to us yet."

"That's comfortin'," Burleigh said. "Where do we go?"

"You all wait here. Stay together," Cale said. "I'm going to do a quick perimeter flight and see how many ways we have out of this chamber. Watch your backs." His short cape flapped behind him as he took his warm glow away from the team.

Maia and Harry plopped down onto the floor, joined after a moment by Burleigh, Michelle, and Tanya. They sat with their backs to each other, watching away from the team instead of into the center of the group. "Harry, you're probably the smartest one of us," Burleigh said. "What do you think is goin' on here?"

"Well . . . I do have a theory, actually." Harry yawned. "I don't suppose any of you have any energy drinks or coffee or anything? I'm dying for a shot of caffeine right now."

"I've got a chocolate bar," Maia said. "I could share it around, yeah?"

"Girl, you just spoke the magic words," Michelle said. "It won't stop me hurting, but a bite of chocolate would go a long way to improving my outlook." She coughed and wheezed. Harry looked concerned but said nothing.

"Yes, please," Tanya said. "Is something normal and wonderful in this terrible place."

Maia carefully unwrapped the bar and broke it into sections, saving one for Cale. She passed the pieces around. They were barely a bite apiece, but the way they all savored them, it was as if they were enjoying the most expensive designer desserts from a five-star restaurant.

"That is just what I needed," Burleigh said. "What's your theory, Harry?"

"Aliens," Harry said.

"Bullshit," Michelle said, and everyone laughed. "Oh, oh ow. Don't make me laugh." Her laugh turned into a cough that hurt her enough for tears to squeeze from the corners of her eyes.

"Then don't say somethin' funny," Burleigh said.

"We already know aliens exist. The Hind, and the races that they apparently have encountered beyond our solar system."

"You think this is Hind installation?" Tanya asked.

"No. I think it's older. Much older. Maybe millions of years if those are actual dinosaurs in the tanks."

Maia shivered. "So these aliens have been . . . torturing things for millions of years? That's messed up."

"I don't think it's torture. At least, not what we think of as torture. There was too much similarity in the growths coming out of each corpse. The legs. The mouth feature. I think they were trying to grow a specific creature, and I think it was one of them. The aliens."

"I do not understand," Tanya said. Maia was glad someone else had said it first, because she didn't follow either.

Harry gestured like a professor from the Hero Academy as he tried to put his theory into words that would make sense to the rest of the team. "Say you're going to colonize other star systems and there was no way for you to go faster than the speed of light, or to warp space the way the Hind do. It would take thousands of years to cover the distances, and maybe generation ships aren't practical. So you get creative. You send out lots and lots of ships. Small, fast ones, packed with nanotech and data. Most of them won't survive the trip. They'll get sucked into stars or find systems with no useful planets. Some will make it to viable worlds, and if they survive landing—or crashing, if you like—then they set about the process of colonizing."

"How can they colonize a planet if there aren't any . . ." Burleigh stopped, looking over at one of the tanks. "They're trying to modify animals into themselves. The spider things must have been looking for . . . for . . ."

"Hosts," Harry said. "Yes, maybe for millions of years. They're working on a long-term plan. They build this base, however long it takes, using native resources. When it's ready, they start examining local fauna to find one they can adapt into their native race. I assume once they've found a way to recreate their own race, it's just a matter of making a large enough seed population to self-perpetuate. Throw in all the accumulated information and technology they sent along in the original ship and they've got an invading species with advanced technological capabilities. It's the slowest, most insidious invasion ever. The planet's inhabitants might never know they've been invaded until it's too late."

"Too late for what? Is that chocolate?" Cale landed beside the group.

"We saved you a piece," Maia said.

"Harry was just tellin' us we've stumbled upon ground zero for an invasion of the Earth."

"I . . . what?" Cale frowned. "Harry, you better tell me what you told them." He listened as Harry reiterated his theory. Instead of immediately discounting it as far-fetched or accepting it as gospel, he merely nodded. "All right. We'll see if that's what it turns out to be and if so, we'll address it at that time."

"How are we gonna *address it*, Cale?" Burleigh asked quietly. "Tell 'em thanks but no thanks? Build a border wall?"

"Nuke them from orbit," Tanya suggested. "Is only way to be sure. I have seen that movie."

"We're not doing anything until we know what's going on," Cale said. "And that's final."

"Did you find a way out?" Maia asked.

"I found two other exits from this chamber." Cale pointed diagonally off to the left and then to the right. "I don't know where either of them lead." He realized he was still holding the piece of chocolate Maia had offered him and ate it. "Anybody want to make a guess?"

"I don't know. Left?" Burleigh suggested. "Then we just keep goin' left until we either circle back or find the way out."

Cale nodded. "Makes as much sense as anything else in this place. Let's get out of here."

Chapter Fifteen

From Maia's playlist: "Electric" - <u>The Church</u>

The new corridor was exactly like the one they'd left except for different tanked animal corpses. The last two tanks bothered her more than many of the others had and she wasn't sure why. Even the Neanderthal-looking woman they'd found didn't upset her the way the rabbit had. It was just a basic snow bunny, caught somewhere between its winter white and summer mottled brown, but it had a full set of five well-formed insectoid legs growing from its abdomen, a pair of pincers emerging from its shoulders, and the petal-mouth thing growing from its back. Its pelt peeled away to reveal carapace beneath, and it gave all of them a much clearer idea of the intended end result of the disturbing flesh modifications.

The other tank that bothered Maia held a bottlenose dolphin. It had no legs like so many of the others but its jaw was wrenched open to show possibly an entire head instead of just the petal mouth. The head was roughly spherical and about the size of a cantaloupe. The petals were clenched into a conical beak protruding from the front of the head. Although most of the other creatures that displayed the petals had them peeled back to show their layered teeth, the dolphin's mutation showed the back side, with interlocking armor plates like those of an armadillo. The way the mouth came to a sharp point, Harry suggested it could probably be used like a spear point. "Whatever else these things are, they certainly seem to be apex predators."

It wasn't readily apparent what killed the dolphin. Perhaps it starved to death or even drowned. The way the head and mouth of the other creature grew from the dolphin's throat like a cancer made Maia gag, nearly puking up her bite of chocolate. The only reason she hadn't done so was because somewhere, deep down, she knew it might be the last chocolate she'd ever have and wasn't willing to part with it so easily.

Michelle was not doing well. Her pain level was increasing until not only could she not walk, she whimpered when Burleigh accidentally jostled her while carrying her. Silent tears rolled down her cheeks as she soldiered on, trying to beat the pain by sheer force of will. Harry and Cale had a quiet conversation out of everyone else's earshot, and Maia suspected Michelle was the subject. They wouldn't leave her behind, of course, Just Cause didn't do that, but her injuries were taking a toll on all of them, and sooner or later, if they didn't get her some real medical attention, she was going to get much worse. Michelle coughed constantly. Her breathing was labored and had developed a bubbly quality that made Maia think maybe she had a punctured lung.

Maia hung her head as she walked. Michelle's broken ribs were her fault, and if Michelle died from complications of those injuries, that would weigh on Maia for a long time. What was the point of saving a life if the lifesaving process ultimately killed the victim? She knew she shouldn't be thinking that way. She'd saved Michelle from drowning, and she couldn't have simply let the young woman die in the water. That would be inhumane. While Michelle lived, there still a chance they could find some medical supplies or find a way out and call for help.

"Hey, Michelle, are you hearing any radio signals? Any chance you can send a broadband call for help on all frequencies?" Maia asked.

"No and no." Michelle coughed and winced. Blood flecked her lips. "Quiet down here." She managed a smile. "You know how rare it is for me to experience radio silence? Maybe I should—" She coughed. "—Move to a cave."

"That's actually good information," Harry said. "Electrical motors and unshielded cables create radio interference. It's like a persistent hum, from what Michelle has told me. It means all this luminescent material isn't electric."

"How's it glowin' then?" Burleigh asked.

"I have no idea. Chemical or radiation, maybe," Harry said.

"So we get lethal radiation doses," Tanya said. "Very comforting."

"We don't know that's the case," Cale said.

"We do not know it is not." Tanya paced back and forth, arms clenched tightly around herself.

Almost without any warning, they found a door in the side of the corridor. It was in a section where the wall luminescence was largely dark, and unlike the cell doors they'd opened to escape, this one was scarred by a patina of rust and salt corrosion. "Should we open it?" Maia asked. She dug out the spider leg she'd used as a key to free the others.

"Yes, absolutely," Cale said. "As few branches as we've found, anything could be important."

"Well, now, maybe we need to rethink this," Harry said. "Rust comes from moisture, and salt corrosion makes me think this door might be shut for a very good reason. There might be ocean behind it. If we open it, we could flood this whole complex if we're beneath the water line."

"Or we could escape," Tanya said. "I think we should open it. Please."

"You think if the ocean floods in here we can all just swim to safety?" Michelle snorted, then coughed out more blood flecks. "You might as well snap my neck now to save time."

"I, uh . . ." Burleigh glanced at Maia. She wondered if he was about to admit his inability to swim. "I don't want to drown everyone here. Maybe Maia could get out if there's a clear path to the surface, but what does that solve if everyone else is dead?

"Plus, there's still a hurricane up there, yeah? At least, it's probably not done yet." Maia shrugged. "Even if I could get up to the surface, I'm not going to do much good without a boat and a radio. I can still drown too if I can't get to the surface in time." Tanya's face fell and Maia knew she'd crushed her friend's spirit.

Cale looked at the others, a struggle on his face. Maia could see the hope turning to dismay as he weighed the options and decided that the risk was too great. "No, you all are right. We keep going, for now. If we don't find another way out, we come back here and try this anyway."

"Fuck you all!" Tanya cried, and ran down the corridor.

Cale brightened his glow. "I'll go after her."

"No, let me," Maia said. "Girl talk, yeah?"

She followed after Tanya, who hadn't run very far despite her ability to cover miles in seconds. Tanya knelt in the middle of the corridor, halfway between the door and the chamber of corpses. Her fists were balled up and her head was bowed forward.

"Tanya . . ." Maia stood over the Russian for a moment, then sat down on the floor beside her.

The speedster looked up at her in the near darkness. The corridor glow reflected off the tears tracking down the girl's cheeks. "This is hell, Maia. We will never escape. We will die here."

"Hey, you don't know that, yeah? We're superheroes. We're going to be okay."

"You do not know that either." Tanya sniffled and wiped her nose with the back of her gloved hand. "We can wander for hours here and never find another path. Michelle is dying. Soon the rest of us will. Then they can put us into tanks."

"Who?"

"The aliens. Harry's aliens. The ones who have made this place."

"There might not *be* any aliens, Tanya. Maybe just those spider things, and they're just machines. They didn't do anything to us except bring us back here. Nobody's stopped us since we got out. It's just robots following a . . . a million year old program without knowing what to do next."

"I hope you are right, Maia, but I fear otherwise." Tanya shuddered.

Maia embraced her. "I'm sorry this is how things are going. We should be back home watching movies and eating popcorn."

Tanya laughed, one quick, bitter chuckle. "I do not like popcorn."

"How can you not like popcorn? It's like, nature's perfect movie snack, yeah?"

"It gets stuck in my teeth."

"I'll bring extra toothpicks."

Maia helped Tanya to her feet and the two girls returned to the rest of the team, who were sitting and resting against the corridor wall.

"Everythin' okay now?" Burleigh asked them.

"*Da*," Tanya said.

"Good enough," Maia added. "Let's get going. Somewhere there has to be a way out. Those spider things had to leave and come back."

They journeyed onward, mostly in silence but for Michelle's tortured breathing and juicy coughs.

Shortly, they happened upon another door. This one was on the opposite side of the corridor, and seemed to be unharmed by rust or salt corrosion. "Now that looks more promising," Harry said. "I think we open this one. Any opposed?"

Nobody was, so Maia stepped up with the spider leg, unrolled it, and poked the tip into the conical hole. The door unlatched and she swung it open to reveal a storage room full of supplies.

Clothing, tools, packs . . . all thrown into haphazard piles as if they'd been determined important enough to keep but not important enough to examine and catalog.

Maia even saw an entire kayak made of wood and lined with skin lying on its side. Maybe it had belonged to the woman who they had found in the tank in the corpse chamber, or maybe it was from someone they hadn't seen. "Fan out, look for medical supplies," Cale ordered.

The heroes spread out, each searching through a portion of the salvage. It looked like maybe sufficient gear for seven or eight people. Most of it was modern clothing and Maia thought it might have come from the crew of the *Atlanta Nights*. Quilted clothing, thermal underwear, parkas and sweatshirts. Boots and socks. All of them were crusted with sea salt and smelled as if they'd been worn recently. They had all been neatly slit for easy removal.

Then Burleigh gasped and everyone crowded around to see what he held up for display: a small blue and white outfit that had until recently been worn by their team leader Sara. "They took her body," he said, tears in his eyes. "That's not right."

"We'll try to find her," Cale said. "Pack up her costume. We should bring it back with us."

Maia felt a tiny glimmer of hope at the way he said it, as if them returning safely was a foregone conclusion. "I'll take it." She held her hand out to Burleigh. "I've got room in my pouch and it won't slow me down."

Burleigh handed it to her. "Make sure it gets back home, kid."

"I will." Maia rolled it up and stowed it in the bottom of her pouch.

"She had a pack and lots of gear. Is it here?" Harry asked.

Tanya found Sara's pack. In it they found a fully stocked medical kit, an undamaged radio and emergency beacon, flares and flare gun, emergency rations and water, another multitool like Maia's, a thermal blanket, and chemical handwarmers. Harry immediately went into the emergency kit and checked the stock of injectable painkillers. "Four," he said. "I'm using one on Michelle right now."

She winced when the needle went in, but looked relieved afterward. "Thanks . . . Don't waste too much on me."

"Nonsense. It's not a waste to keep you comfortable. You're part of this team, and you need it more than anyone else here. Besides, we're going to need someone who can call for help, and who better than our own human radio?" Nobody questioned Harry taking charge of the medical kit. He adjusted the straps on Sara's backpack as long as they would go and slipped it over his shoulders, keeping the handwarmers, water, and rations in addition to the medical kit. Burleigh got the flare gun and extra magazines for it. Everyone else got one of the regular flares except for Michelle, who got the radio and beacon.

Tanya found a pistol amid the gear that probably came from the *Atlanta Nights'* crew. It was a semi-automatic with a full clip of twelve shots. "I will take this if nobody else will," she said. "My training included firearms."

"Keep it," Cale said. "You're probably the best shot with it anyway."

"Guys!" Michelle's strong warning devolved into more coughing.

Everyone spun around to see a metallic spider the size of a toddler in the doorway.

Chapter Sixteen

From Maia's playlist: "Secrets" - Tears for Fears

Weapons came up—Tanya's pistol, Burleigh's axe. Maia crouched, ready to leap into action, even though her previous experience with fighting the spiders had been an abject failure. Cale rose off the ground, brightening himself so his team could see well enough to fight. Harry, whose abilities were useless without a reserve of ice on hand, stood between Michelle and the spider, ready to defend her with open hands if required.

The spider didn't move.

The team hesitated as well. Tensions ran so high Maia could practically feel the air of the room vibrating with barely restrained aggression, but nobody made the first move. Feeling awkward, she glanced up at Cale. "What do we do?"

"I . . . don't know."

"It's like it's waitin' for somethin'," Burleigh said. "Reinforcements, maybe?"

Burleigh stepped forward. "Stay behind me, kid. You're the second line of defense." He hefted his axe.

As he approached the spider, it finally responded, but instead of charging at him or fleeing, it lowered its body to the floor and actually raised its five feet into the air.

"It looks like it's surrendering, yeah?" Maia said.

"I don't know," Burleigh said. He took another step toward the thing and it waved its foot appendages as if encouraging them to see it. He took another step and raised his axe in preparation for smashing the spider into oblivion.

Even threatened by the axe, it remained unmoving, legs raised in supplication. Burleigh lowered his axe and tapped it against the spider. Maia held her breath, nerves racing. The spider let Burleigh poke it several times, then sweep it back using the axe head like a hockey stick.

"I don't get it," Burleigh said, glancing back at the others. "Before, they were all over us. Now there's just one and it's playin' nice?"

"They didn't stop us from escaping," Cale said. "And we've been able to go wherever we wished. We even found supplies and weapons. I think maybe our hosts want to talk to us."

Tanya snorted. "You would make peace with these monsters who kill and maim?" She considered the pistol she still held. "I would shoot it if I thought it would make any difference, but I will not waste a bullet."

"Stand down, Tanya. That's an order. Burleigh, give me some space." Cale dropped to the floor before the spider. "All right, here's your chance. I'm listening."

The spider pulled its legs inside its body and extended a single limb up from its center. The limb resembled a human hand, albeit with overlong fingers and too many joints. It made what Maia thought was an unmistakable follow-me gesture, then drew the limb back and slowly extended its legs once more.

"That's odd. That's a human gesture," Harry said. "Maybe they've had more interactions with humans than I thought."

"We only saw the one woman in the, uh, tanks," Burleigh said. "Maybe they stopped after that?"

"Or they figured out how to make it work for humans," Tanya said.

Burleigh raised the axe, ready to strike. Maia tensed, not knowing what to do next, but the spider backed up a few feet and stopped. "Easy, everyone," Cale said. He took a couple steps toward the spider and stopped. It backed up again stopping in the doorway of the chamber.

"I do not trust this," Tanya said. "It is a trick."

"I'm with the Russkie on this," Burleigh said. "I think we're better findin' our own way."

"As easily as they overran us at the lifeboat, I'm inclined to think they could do so again here if that was their intent. This thing is trying a different tactic. Maybe it's a trap, but maybe it's also progress toward getting out of here." Cale sighed. "I've decided. We follow it."

Tanya stamped her foot but said nothing else.

Moving with the utmost caution, the team followed the spider into the corridor, where they found yet another unexpected event. They had previously experienced the spiders' ability to transport them by encapsulating them in the liquid metal bodies. Now, a large group of the spiders had formed themselves into something resembling a holiday sleigh, if a sleigh had dozens of tiny legs beneath it instead of runners and a cheerful old horse to pull it. Maia wondered if they'd seen one before somehow.

"Far out . . ." Michelle's voice was faint and slurred from the painkillers in her system.

Burleigh shook his head. "Uh-uh. Nope. This is all wrong. We're not lettin' them lead us around by our noses, are we, Cale?"

Cale floated into the air above the sleigh. "Sorry, Burleigh, but for now that's exactly what we're doing. We don't know where we are and Michelle needs medical treatment. I don't know if that's something that will be on the table, but we have to try."

"All that gear we found might belong to the crew of the *Atlanta Nights*," Maia said. "Don't we have an obligation to find out what happened to them and if they're still alive? With the ship being abandoned like it was and that spider on board, don't you think they were probably taken the same way we were? They're probably in this base somewhere."

"Unless they are already infected by whatever it is that makes them grow insect legs," Tanya said. "Please, there must be another way."

Cale extended his hand to her. "Tanya, believe me, if there was anything else I felt we could do right now, we would be doing that. Michelle is in bad shape. If we can get her some kind of help, that has to be of the utmost importance."

"He's not wrong, Tanya," Harry said. "She's got a punctured lung. If her breathing gets much worse, I'm going to have to decompress her chest, and this is hardly what I'd call a sterile environment."

"All right. All is wonderful. Everybody will be fine." Tanya pushed past the others, visibly steeled herself, then stepped up onto the metal sleigh.

Maia slipped onto the bench beside her and patted her friend's leg. "It'll be okay, yeah? We'll figure it out."

Burleigh carefully sat Michelle between him and Harry on the second seat while Cale hovered overhead. "Okay, this is what you wanted," he said to what Maia thought of as *their* spider. "We're all here. Take us to where you want us to go."

The movement of the sleigh was smooth, almost as if it were traveling on runners after all instead of feet. The spider that had first approached them trotted ahead of the sleigh as if it were a dog. Maia found the mechanics of a five-legged creature's gait fascinating. Its legs were a blur and the sleigh went fast enough that Cale had to grab hold of it to keep from being left behind. They raced down featureless pentagonal corridors, lit only by the luminescent material in the walls. Sometimes it was dark for large sections, making Maia wonder if they were saving power for unused areas, or if they were just in poor repair. Were the spiders keeping up the whole base or were they focusing their attention elsewhere?

Burleigh leaned forward from the rear seat. "How fast you think we're goin', Tanya?"

"Hard to say without me running too. Maybe a hundred, hundred twenty kilometers per hour."

"I can't believe this base is so big and so deserted," Harry said. "Whoever built it had some pretty grandiose plans."

"You mean your aliens, yeah?" Maia asked. "You still think it's aliens?"

"Yes, I do."

The sleigh slowed as they approached another chamber, this one lit not by the blue-white wall luminescence, but by the comforting and familiar orange flicker of firelight. They emerged from the corridor into a room that looked like it had been transported right out of a European castle, with walls shaped like stone blocks. Unlike the corridors with the pentagonal cross section, this room had vertical walls. Tapestries hung along the wall, showing meaningless geometric shapes instead of traditional scenes. Carpets decorated the stone floor and a large fireplace formed the centerpiece of one wall, with a stonework mantle above and several chairs forming a semicircle around the hearth. End tables held crystal goblets of liquid while candelabras and sconces added their own natural illumination to the room.

The sleigh halted and the team dismounted. As Maia watched, the liquid metal creation broke apart into dozens of spiders like the one that had first encouraged them to follow, and they fled back into the corridor, metal legs clicking on the stone floors.

The floor felt funny under Maia's feet, and she might not have noticed if her boots had been hard-soled like the others. Hers were soft so she could swim in them, and that's why she noticed that the rug wasn't soft. It wasn't fibrous at all, in fact. She was pretty sure it was rock or metal and was only colored to look like a rug. "This is weird," she said. "It only looks soft, but it's as hard as everything else."

"Same with tapestries," Tanya said after trotting to the wall to check. "Is not cloth."

"The candle flames and fireplace are generating heat, but I don't see any smoke, and I don't think anything is actually burning," Harry said.

"It's like someone only ever saw pictures of it," Cale said.

"Maybe . . . they did." Michelle coughed and wheezed. She looked pale beneath her natural exotic skin color. "Movies or TV."

Harry pulled out the stethoscope from the first aid kit and listened to Michelle's chest. "I don't like the sound of that. Her chest cavity is filling up with air. We have to decompress her to release the pressure."

"Guys . . ." Burleigh's voice was soft but loaded with warning implications. "We're not alone."

Chapter Seventeen

From Maia's playlist: "Red Right Hand"
- Nick Cave & The Bad Seeds

The team's weapons came to bear upon a figure who stood from where he had been sitting in one of the chairs before the fireplace. He was tall and muscular like Burleigh, but with a skin tone that suggested he was native to the region. He had a thatch of thick, black hair and a full beard. He wore ill-fitting, contemporary clothing that seemed fit to burst at the seams from his musculature. His deep set eyes regarded the team with a mixture of curiosity and amusement.

"Hello," he said after the team had a chance to really look at him. "I am Tlalit. Welcome to my home."

Cale glanced at the others. "I'm Midnight Sun. I'm the leader of this team." He proceeded to introduce the rest of the group, something which was thoroughly Canadian in its politeness, but nevertheless made Maia uncomfortable. It felt wrong, giving away information to a potential enemy. On the other hand, no overt hostility had been directed toward them—not even when they were fighting off the spiders at the lifeboat. None of them had actually been hurt by anything except the helicopter crash and the events immediately after. Perhaps Tlalit wasn't actually an enemy.

Then Maia noticed his shoes were on the wrong feet. It was a small detail, but once she'd seen it, she couldn't look away. It was another incorrect detail, like the rugs that weren't actually rugs and the tapestries that weren't actually tapestries. She wondered if anything in the room was real or if it was all stage dressing to cover up something more sinister. Maybe Tlalit was as fake as everything else.

"Please, you all seem tired. Come warm yourselves by my hearth," Tlalit said. His voice was a powerful baritone, like a television or radio announcer, but despite his native appearance, he had the same bland accent that every newscaster used, like he had learned it from watching TV. "Would you care for some refreshments?"

"We're fine, thank you," Cale said. "Why are we here?"

Tlalit tilted his head sideways a few degrees, like a curious dog. "I have saved your lives."

"We were doin' just fine, thanks," Burleigh said. "We didn't ask to get hauled in here and locked up in your jail."

"Jail?" Tlalit looked confused. "Perhaps you mean the isolation chambers? I had to be sure none of you carried a contagious disease. I am very isolated here in this place, and have no . . . what is the word? *Resistance* to modern diseases."

"None of us are sick," Cale said. "Although my companion Simulcast is injured. Do you have medical facilities here?"

"Yes, of course," Tlalit said. "Do you wish me to have her brought to them? I can recall the rovers."

Rover was a good name for the spider things, Maia thought. Somehow it made them seem less sinister. Maybe it was because she associated *rover* with the name for a dog. Were they simply loyal pets? Their behavior had suggested they followed orders but didn't show much initiative except in the following of those orders.

"No, not yet," Cale said. "It's important that we stay all together."

"Of course."

"What did you mean, *modern diseases*?" Harry asked. "Just how old are you, and how old is this place? And for that matter, *who* are you?"

Tlalit did the head-tilt again. "As I have said, I am Tlalit. That is who I am. Please, come sit with me and we will talk."

The team crossed the room. The fire was real, although up close, Maia decided Harry had been correct in his assessment that it wasn't burning any kind of actual wood. The chairs were as fake as everything else in the room—hard as rocks and quite possibly made from them. She sat on one, as did the others on the team, but stayed right on the edge, ready to jump up if needed. She didn't know if they would be called upon to fight or to do something else, but she wanted to be ready to act.

"Would you care for refreshments?" Tlalit asked again, and held up a crystal goblet with some kind of liquid in it.

"No thank you. We brought our own," Cale said.

"Very well. I will do my best to answer your questions, although I have some limits to my vocabulary. It is only recently that I have been able to receive signals at all."

"Why couldn't you before?" Harry asked.

"The volume of ice above us has been too great."

"And all this—" Cale waved his hand at the room around them. "Is from receiving our transmissions?"

"Yes."

"Can you make it possible for us to send and receive our own transmissions?" Cale asked, looking in Michelle's direction.

"There is a large and powerful atmospheric disturbance that is interfering with my equipment."

"Maybe we can help you fix it if you show us," Burleigh said.

"I do not believe you would comprehend my technology. It is . . . different than yours."

"So you're not from around here." Burleigh made it a statement instead of a question.

Tlalit smiled as if it was something he'd practiced in a mirror. "I am a native of this world."

Harry's smile was one of vindication. "Nobody says that, Tlalit. You're an alien, aren't you?"

"I am not from a different world."

"What about all those . . . hybrids in the big chamber?" Harry asked.

"They are also native to this world."

"Bullshit," Tanya said.

"How long have you been down here, Tlalit?" Cale asked.

"It is . . . hard to tell. There is no way to mark the passage of time below the surface. I believe it to be a long time. It was a time when there was far less ice above. Time is not of great importance to . . . my people."

"And who are they? I still don't believe you're human," Harry said.

"This . . . form cannot reproduce the sounds to identify them. They are very old, very wise."

Maia snorted. All her life, she'd been taught that wisdom and age went hand in hand, but she'd met plenty of youthful folks who were wise, and plenty of elderly who were so narrow-minded and stuck in their ways that they were more foolish than anything else.

"And they've been down here a very long time?" Cale asked.

"Not *they*. They are not here at all. They would not have survived the journey here."

Harry crossed his arms. "I'm thinking my theory was pretty close to accurate. What about your hybrids? What is the reason for them?"

"It has been our challenge to find a way to modify this world's forms to find one that will be . . . compatible."

"Compatible with *what*? Those insect parts? What the hell are you tryin' to do?" Burleigh slapped his hands on his knees.

"We are trying to do what all life seeks to do," Tlalit said. "Survive."

"So what happens now?" Cale asked. "What does your *survival* mean for the rest of us?"

Maia guessed that by *the rest of us* he meant the entire human race, not just the members of JCAC.

"It is my hope we can come to . . . an understanding." Tlalit's smile was so artificial it looked like it was painted onto his face by an amateur artist.

"We're going to need to talk this over," Cale said, looking like he'd just swallowed a bite of something rotten.

Tlalit nodded. "Of course."

* * *

"I hate it when I'm right." Harry paced back and forth in what passed for Tlalit's medical facility. Their host had generously offered it to them to assist in treating Michelle and then given them some privacy so they could work with his equipment. Why he had departed was anybody's guess, and it had made all of them uncomfortable. The room's equipment was strangely analog, with nothing resembling digital displays or electronics. From what Maia could tell, most of the equipment seemed to have been made from the same liquid metal as the spiders. Perhaps it was made *of* the spiders, given their ability to reshape themselves.

"First time I've ever heard you complain about it," Burleigh said. He'd helped with the procedure to release the air pressure from Michelle's thoracic cavity which had immediately improved her breathing. She was sleeping on a metal platform, her head resting on Harry's rolled-up parka.

"I was just guessing!" Harry shouted. "How did I know that they actually *are* aliens?"

"Harry," Cale said softly. "You're going to wake Michelle. She needs the rest."

Harry stopped his pacing and came back to the others. "They're listening in. You know they are."

Burleigh shrugged. "Not much we can do about it."

Harry lowered his voice. "Look, that one room with all the corpses, it was full of all kinds of animals, and even that Neanderthal woman. The one thing we didn't see? Us. Modern humans. Why do you think that is?"

"Because we are . . . compatible," Tanya said. She sat on another platform, kicking her feet in a glum, listless way.

Harry pointed at her. "Right. I figure this place has been buried under the ice for millennia. Global warming isn't just thawing out Arctic sea routes. It uncovered this place, and Tlalit sent his rovers out to find more compatible beings."

"They're not going to find many," Cale said. "Not here on the roof of the world."

"They don't have to find a lot," Harry said. "Tlalit might not have those five legs or weird-ass mouth thing, but I bet his DNA isn't human any longer. He's some kind of weird hybrid thing. They've been waiting here for maybe millions of years. You think they don't know how to be patient? They grab a person here, a ship's crew there, and eventually they get enough people to build another one of these bases. Somewhere else, where there's a much larger population."

"An invasion," Cale said. "Jesus."

"I bet our buddy Tlalit is a hell of a lot older than he looks. As rare as grabbing people must have been until recently, I'm sure they figured out a way to stop aging." Harry gave an acrid laugh. "Who wants to live forever?"

"So what must we do?" Tanya asked. "How can we fight this?"

"We've got to destroy this base. Like, completely destroy it," Maia said.

"How do we do that?" Burleigh asked. "It'd take you and me years to tear it apart piece by piece, and they're not going to just let us do it."

"We're underground," Maia said. "Harry could do it."

Harry shook his head. "I can't fill this place with ice. I don't know how big it is, and my powers have a limited range."

"No, you don't have to fill it with ice," Maia said. "There's a whole ocean up there somewhere, yeah? Fill it with that and then you cap it off with as much ice as you can pile on top of it."

"That's a good idea, kid," Burleigh said. "Only problem is we don't have any way to get the water here, and we don't know which way is out."

"Also, they are not going to let us do it," Tanya said.

Maia crossed her arms. "What, are we just giving up then? Wait for them to—to do whatever they're going to do to us?"

"No, of course not," Cale said. "It is a good idea, Maia, and we'll consider it if we get the opportunity. For now, though, the most important thing is we get Michelle to safety."

"What about the crew of the *Atlanta Nights*?" Maia asked. "Don't you think they're here too?"

Harry snapped his fingers. "Ah, shit. We've got to find them too."

"I can take you to them, but you won't like what you find," said a voice that was instantly familiar yet horribly wrong.

Sara stood across the room from them.

Chapter Eighteen

From Maia's playlist: "Going, Going, Gone" - <u>Bob Dylan</u>

Maia started toward Sara, but Burleigh grabbed her arm and held her back. "Hold on, kid. She's dead and we all know that."

"Maybe was our mistake," Tanya said, but neither did she rush toward their erstwhile leader.

"Sara?" Cale rose into the air to get a better look. Her costume was balled up inside Maia's pack. Instead, she wore a garment of thin, reflective metal, as if she'd fashioned a insulated space blanket into a choirboy-style robe.

Or, Maia reflected, perhaps it was made of the same liquid metal as the spiders.

"Hello, Cale," Sara said.

"How are, uh, how are you feeling?"

"I'm recovering," Sara said. She looked down at herself, wrinkling her brow at her outfit as if she hadn't realized she was wearing it. "That's funny. I don't remember . . ." She looked up at her teammates. "I don't remember wearing this."

"Sara, I'm not sure how to sugar-coat this, so I'm just going to say it. You were dead. You died in the lifeboat. How is it you're here now?" Harry asked.

Sara shrugged. "Near as I can figure it, the machines in this place must have brought me back to life. I sort of remember being on the lifeboat, but it's really vague. I don't remember dying at all, but I'm not sure that's the kind of thing anyone would remember. I awakened a few minutes ago in a nearby room. I overheard you all talking and came to see you."

"She's not talkin' like Sara at all," Burleigh said. "I think we're bein' had."

"We know they took her body," Cale said. "And we know they do a lot with genetics. It's possible they may have reanimated her if she wasn't too far gone."

Sara raised her hand. "I'm right here."

"Why would they do that?" Maia asked.

"They're looking for compatibility. She's probably just as compatible as the rest of us," Harry said.

"Still right here," Sara said.

"It is another trick," Tanya said. "They ask us to trust her. Why let her come to us now if not to gain our trust?"

"Yo, I said I am right. Fucking. Here!" Sara stamped her foot.

"That sounds more like the Sara we know." Cale held his hands out. "I'm sorry, Sara. We're not intentionally ignoring you. There's a lot of extenuating circumstances right now, and Tanya is right. The only reason Tlalit would have sent you to us is to gain our trust."

"Who's Tlalit? Sounds like an Inuit name," Sara said.

"He's our human host. Well, human-ish," Harry said. "I'm pretty sure he's a human-alien hybrid." He paused. "And I'm pretty sure you are too, by now."

"Human . . . alien? You mean like the Hind?" Sara asked.

"No, like an ancient race trying to conquer us at a genetic level."

"And you think I'm one of them?"

"No offense meant, Sara," Burleigh said. "But you were dead and now you're not. That's just not normal."

Sara looked at the others. "Then you're right not to trust me. I formally abdicate my leadership of this team."

"So you have no idea who Tlalit is? But you know where the crew of the *Atlanta Nights* is?" Cale asked.

"No, I haven't seen anyone here besides you and them. Oh, and these funky metal spider things. They're all over the place in the other room. They turn themselves into machines. It's fucking wild."

"Did they . . . do anything to you?" Maia asked. "Put anything inside you?"

"Put something . . ." Sara's voice twisted up in confusion. "What do you mean, *inside me*?"

Cale looked at the others, helplessness sprawled across his features. Maia understood his discomfort. How did they tell Sara that not only had the mysterious technology somehow revived her from death, but she might be sprouting insectoid legs and chitin at any moment?

"It doesn't matter," Harry said. "Not now. What matters now is we get ourselves and the *Atlanta Nights* crew to safety. Sara, do you know the way out of here?"

"No, but I know where the missing crew are. Perhaps one of them knows the way out," Sara said. "We can talk to them when they wake up. Follow me. Uh, please," she added when she remembered she was no longer in charge.

When they wake up. Maia wondered what was being done to them that required them to be . . . not awake.

"Follow Sara," Cale said. He lowered his voice. "Be on your guard."

They followed Sara into the corridor. Maia saw her robe tug at her. It was subtle, and happened so quickly she wasn't certain she'd seen it at all until Sara turned the same direction as the tug.

"Did you see that?" Maia asked Tanya in a low voice.

"*Da*," Tanya said. "She is not in control of herself."

"Do you think she's even alive?"

Tanya shook her head. "This is a trap for us."

"Why go to the trouble? We're already in here, yeah?"

"I do not know."

Burleigh carried Michelle, because Cale said under no circumstances were they to leave her anywhere by herself.

Sara led them to another chamber, about the size of the JCAC hangar. It was pentagonal, with a flat floor but the ceiling raised to a point at room's center. A tall crystalline structure dropped from the ceiling's zenith to stop several feet above the floor, where it was wrapped in a complicated device formed from liquid metal. Arms extended from the metal vertex to hover over six nude human males lying face down on raised platforms. Cables hung from the arms, ending in dozens of thin needles embedded in the men's backs.

"This is why I said you won't be happy," Sara said. "Whatever is going on, these guys are in the middle of it."

"It might be dangerous to remove them," Cale said. "We don't know what this procedure entails."

"Looks kind of like gene therapy," Harry said. "This must be how they are combining alien DNA with human. Did they do this to you, Sara?"

"I don't know."

Tanya pushed past Sara to look more closely at the victims. "These men are alive. You do not think we can free them?"

Harry shook his head. "We could kill them if we interrupt the process at a crucial moment. Still, we may have to if it's the only way to get them out of here."

"Maybe we can help them afterwards, yeah?" Maia asked. "I don't see any spaces for us. Maybe that's why they're not in any hurry to deal with us."

"Could be," Burleigh said. "Limited resources."

Maia looked around the room. Something was missing and she wasn't sure what until she looked back toward Sara. "Hey, Sara, where did you wake up? There are only six platforms in here and they're all full. I don't see any other equipment."

Sara looked around as well. Confusion took over her face. "I—I'm not sure, actually. I thought it was in here because I remember these men, but now I'm not sure. Why can't I remember?"

"You were dead," Harry said. "Who knows how that affects your short-term memory processing?" He looked up at the crystalline structure at the room's center. "This looks more like the material that's in the walls."

"The glowing stuff?" Tanya asked.

"Yes, the glowing stuff. This is more concentrated. It seems like it might be a source of energy, or more directly connected to the main power source. I wonder if it might be vulnerable to interference." Harry bent down to look at one of the men on the platforms. "Or if cutting off the power might stop what's happening here."

"I thought you didn't want to interrupt it, yeah?" Maia asked.

Harry shrugged. "I don't, but we're going to have to take what we can get down here."

Cale nodded. "I agree. Sara, can you still generate ice?"

Sara raised her hand and frowned. A few small snowflakes dropped from her open palm but nothing in the volume they knew she had been capable of when she was alive before. "My powers are gone. Mostly, anyway. Fuck."

"I don't know if that's from you being reanimated or if their treatment has somehow degraded your Musashi gene," Harry said. "I'm strictly an amateur when it comes to this kind of stuff. Once it gets beyond stitching up holes and setting bones, I'm guessing."

"I don't think anybody is an expert on ancient alien technology," Cale said. "However, I'm guessing that the fact we haven't been put into this machine yet or one like it is that Tlalit either doesn't have enough power or enough liquid metal to handle all of us. We've still got to stop him from getting any further."

"If you stop this process, these men will die," Sara said. "I'm sure of that."

"And as soon as it's done with them, the system will be freed up to deal with us," Burleigh said. "Nice little Catch-22. Either we possibly kill the civilians and destroy this machine, or we take the chance that we can destroy it before we ourselves get fed into it."

"Make the call, Cale," Harry said. "What do we do?"

"Don't destroy the machine," Sara said immediately. "It's your only chance to keep these men alive. That's our cardinal mission. Don't forget that."

"Of course she does not want us to destroy the machine," Tanya said. "She is working for them. She is one of them."

"What?" Sara cried. "No, I'm not!"

"That robe she's wearing is made of liquid metal, yeah?" Maia said. "It's dragging her around. She's just a —a puppet."

"No! No, no no!" Sara screamed, and fell to the floor, thrashing like a toddler throwing a tantrum.

"Stay back!" Harry shouted as Tanya and Maia started toward her. They froze in their tracks as Sara continued to scream and roll around.

As suddenly as she'd started, Sara stopped cold and flopped to the floor, unmoving.

The room was so silent Maia could hear the slow breathing of the men on the platforms. Sara, on the other hand, didn't appear to be breathing at all. After a spasmodic episode like she'd just had, her sides should be heaving from the overload of adrenaline in her system. Instead, she lay there, appearing as dead as she should have been.

"Burleigh . . ." Cale's voice was barely a whisper. "Check her."

"Why me?" Burleigh whispered back, but nevertheless he unlimbered his axe and approached Sara. He was the best choice, Maia knew, given his natural strength and toughness, but it was still unnerving to see a man of his size and ability as scared as he was.

With a hand that shook just a little, Burleigh reached out to touch the side of Sara's neck, checking for a pulse. "I think she's . . . really dead this time," he said. He rolled her over onto her back. Her sightless eyes stared up at the ceiling. He reached down to close them.

Her throat split open and the now-familiar toothed petals of the alien orifice burst outward with a hissing squall.

Chapter Nineteen

From Maia's playlist: "Monster / Suicide / America"
- Steppenwolf

With an inhuman hiss, Sara threw Burleigh aside. The liquid metal enrobing her parted, as did flesh beneath, and five insectoid legs burst forth from her hips and abdomen. Her own legs dangled bonelessly but her arms seemed still to function, although the skin split to show chitin underneath and well-formed pincers emerged from her palms.

The Sara-thing scuttled aside, easily dodging an awkward swing from Burleigh's axe. As he drew back for another swing, it rushed him, clenching its upper two legs around him like a linebacker tackling a running back. The pincers closed upon his axe and wrenched it from his grasp.

Maia ran to help Burleigh and the Sara-thing kicked her aside hard enough to send her flying back into one of the metal platforms. It flexed when she hit and tried to flow around her, but Tanya ran over in a blur and strained to pull her free until Maia got her feet under her. Her impact had jarred the man atop it loose and the needles withdrew from him. "Help the civilian," Maia said, and Tanya rushed to do so.

Cale brightened his light to make the interior of the room like daylight. His illumination showed shadowy machinery behind the walls, moving around the exterior. Around the room, the machinery was pulling the needles away from the men of the *Atlanta Nights*.

None of them moved, but the platforms beneath them did. They split and reformed. Some became low, mobile carpets to transport the unconscious civilians away from the danger, while others transformed into empty platforms, presumably awaiting the surviving members of Just Cause Arctic Circle.

Burleigh punched the Sara-thing in its face, trying to dislodge its grip around him as it dragged him toward an empty platform. The petal mouth snapped at his hand, catching it once and dragging its sharp teeth across his skin but unable to penetrate it.

Maia ran back in on the Sara-thing, smashing into it shoulder first and forcing it to release Burleigh. She shrieked as the thing immediately grabbed her waist with its chitinous arms and held her tight in a parody of a hug. She locked her hands around the Sara-thing's human throat, just beneath the petal mouth, and squeezed. The thing wrapped its legs around Maia and tried to drag her toward an empty platform. She dug her heels into the floor and fought back against the insistent tugging.

Harry threw a flare toward the exit. The brilliant pink light bounced into the doorway and stopped, spitting sparks and smoke. The embedded luminous material in the floor and walls that carried the underground base's illumination began to bubble and melt. The liquid metal carpets retreated to the far wall, carrying their unconscious civilian passengers.

Burleigh brought his axe down on one of the Sara-thing's legs and severed it. Red-purple ichor sprayed forth with a stink like a mix of copper and sulfur. The petal-mouth shrieked and the Sara-thing's body twisted into an impossible angle and backhanded Burleigh across the room. He crashed against the wall and a torrent of rotten rock rained around him to reveal a shiny, grainy surface beneath it.

"Permafrost! I can work with that!" Harry shouted, and raised his hands. Tendrils of ice flowed out from the broken wall like the tentacles of some fantastic undersea beast.

Maia wrestled with the wounded Sara-thing. She'd forgotten every last tenet of Mustang Sally's combat training except one thing: *don't fight fair and don't expect others to fight fair; fight to win.* She overcame her revulsion and squeezed the Sara-thing's throat as hard as she could. It wasn't Sara anymore, it was an inhuman monster, and as long as Maia continued to convince herself of that, she found the strength to carry on with the fight. The Sara-thing's eyes bulged and its petal mouth flopped in her face, scratching her with its sharp teeth and hissing its stinking breath. Chitin crackled beneath Maia's fingers and the Sara-thing's grip around her waist loosened. She flung it away from her.

The Sara-thing struggled back onto its four remaining legs. It swayed from its injuries, and what had been Sara's head lolled backward, neck clearly broken from Maia's grip. And somehow, despite all the wounds, it still came after her.

Three gunshots roared through the small room. Two fresh wounds appeared in the Sara-thing's upper torso and its petal-mouth shredded from a third. Tanya stood in a classic shooter's pose, smoking pistol in a two-handed grip, one leg forward and one behind to brace her. Her eyes were wide as searchlights. The Sara-thing screamed in wordless pain and fury until Burleigh brought his axe diagonally across its torso like the lumberjack he was. It bit deep into the Sara-thing's torso, severing her spine and releasing a torrent of shattered chitin and broken organs from the wound.

The Sara-thing fell, unmoving but for a few brief leg twitches. Maia found she was splattered from head to toe with the thing's effluvia. She pushed the corpse off and jumped away before her nausea grew too great.

"Maia, are you all right?" Burleigh shouted at her as she fell to her hands and knees. She was shaking and felt like she was going to throw up. She heard the sounds of material clashing against material but all she could see were her hands on the floor in front of her.

Burleigh knelt beside her, putting a hand between her shoulder blades. "Kid, are you hurt?"

"N-no." Maia closed her eyes for a moment, then sat back on her heels. "I . . . I killed her, Burleigh. I killed Sara."

"No, you didn't. She died in the helicopter crash. That . . . thing . . . that wasn't Sara."

Maia opened her eyes slowly, terrified that the Sara-thing would be in her field of vision, but she didn't see anything except Burleigh's concerned face. "Burleigh . . . I'm so sorry." Tears ran down her cheeks. Burleigh wrapped her in a strong embrace. She buried her face against his shoulder. "I never should have come up here. Everything's gone wrong since I showed up."

"Maia, no. None of this is your fault. The storm, the crash, the fucking aliens. This was going to happen no matter what."

More sounds of materials crashing together penetrated the fog in Maia's brain. "What's happening, Burleigh? What's that noise?"

"That's Harry, doing his thing," Burleigh said. "We're safe, for the moment."

Maia raised her head to look around.

Harry had pulled a lot of ice from the permafrost. He'd used some of it to seal the entrance to the chamber and more of it to wrap up the Sara-thing's body. A floor-to-ceiling wall of ice had trapped all the liquid metal implements in the room and they sloshed back and forth behind it like angry aquarium water. Finally, he'd made a giant upside-down icicle force itself upward to split the crystal column that emerged from the ceiling. It had gone dark, as had all the luminescent material in the room. The only light came from Cale's power, like a dim star at the room's zenith.

The six men from the *Atlanta Nights* lay on the floor, still nude. The realization made Maia's face grow hot, but she knew there wasn't anything available to cover them with. Then she remembered the thermal blanket in her pouch. She disengaged herself from Burleigh's arms and withdrew it. "Here," she said to him. "Maybe you can . . . cover those guys up, yeah?"

"Of course." He took the blanket. "You gonna be okay for a minute?"

"I think so."

Burleigh and Harry moved the six unconscious men close to each other and covered them with the thermal blanket. Cale donated his cape as well. "How are they doing, Harry?"

Harry shook his head. "I don't know. They're alive, but their vital signs are all pretty weak. Interrupting the process like we did may have been a death sentence. I don't know how to save them." He hung his head in exhaustion and dismay.

Tanya clasped one of his hands in hers. "You saw what was done to Sara. It was being done to these men. You cannot save them any more than we could save her. Killing them might be a kindness."

Harry turned to her, a spark in his eyes. "No! We came all the way out here to save them and until they die from complications of . . . whatever was being done to them, or because they turn into five-legged murder machines and we have to put them down . . . we don't let any harm come to them."

"I'm with Harry on this," Cale said. "Until there's no hope of saving them, we have to operate on the assumption that they can be healed from whatever has been done to them. There are a dozen parahuman healers in Just Cause facilities across the U.S. and more in other countries. If we can get them out of here, I believe we can save them."

"That's easier said than done, boss," Burleigh said. "We're not doin' much better than we were before, except now we're stuck with seven wounded instead of just one, and we still don't know where to go."

Maia looked up at the hole in the wall from where Harry had pulled the ice. An idea gnawed at the edges of her mind and she clenched her fists as she tried to force it to come to fruition past the layers of exhaustion threatening to overwhelm her. "Signals," she said at last.

"What's that, Maia?" Cale asked.

"Signals. Tlalit said he had been receiving signals. The spiders were outside. There's a way out, yeah?"

"We already know there's a way out," Harry said. "Unless we know where it is, that isn't really useful."

"No, hear me out. I think there's a limited amount of the liquid metal, yeah? Otherwise they wouldn't have had to wait to try to . . . to feed us into the machine. It's why there aren't any guards and so much of the facility is dark and seems like it's not being used."

Harry's eyes widened. "They don't have enough resources. Even after millions of years, they don't have enough."

"That's probably why they haven't already overrun the planet," Cale said. "This is as much as they've been able to manage."

"Now that they can get to the surface, and they know there's a technologically advanced civilization, they will be able to find resources to fulfill their mission," Harry said. "But what about the signals you mentioned, Maia?"

"You said this stuff that's like glass or plastic works like fiber optic cables. It's carrying power and information and who knows what else, yeah? How about radio signals?"

Everyone looked up at the crystal that had been the foundation for the devices that fed alien DNA into the *Atlanta Nights* crew. Realization dawned on Harry's face. "Oh, shit. We can use it like an antenna!"

Cale nodded. "Thank you, Maia. You may have just given us the key to getting out of here."

Tanya frowned. "Tlalit will try to stop us."

Burleigh slapped his axe into his palm. "Let him."

Chapter Twenty

From Maia's playlist: "Edge of the Ocean" - Ivy

"Michelle? Come on, Michelle, you need to wake up." Harry broke open an ammonia ampoule from the first aid kit and waved it underneath her nose. "Time to work now."

Michelle started, tried to sit up too quickly, and squealed as the ends of her broken ribs grated against each other. Burleigh had her head in his lap and he took her shoulders and eased her back down. "Hang in there, Michelle. We're gonna get help soon, but we need you to use your powers first."

"I can't . . . I can't use my powers," Michelle said. "Hurts too much."

Maia knelt beside her, rubbing one of her wrists. "I know it hurts, and I'm so sorry about that. But we think we've found a way for you to get a transmission outside this base."

"We can call for help," Tanya said, rubbing Michelle's other wrist.

Michelle pulled her hand free of Maia's grasp and batted away Harry's hand with the ammonia inhalant before he could bring it close to her again. Maia caught a whiff of the ammonia and it immediately made her heart pound like she was about to take an oral exam at the Academy. "No, no more. It's hard enough to breathe as it is." She took a shaky breath, paused, then let it out. "Easier than it was, though. Something's stabbing me in the side."

"I had to decompress your chest cavity. The needle is still there, I'm afraid," Harry said. "In case we have to do it again. You've got a collapsed lung." Michelle reached gingerly toward the needle taped against her side but Harry guided her hand away from it. "It's there, trust me. I'm banking on this being a relatively sterile environment this far below the surface. Otherwise I'd be a lot more worried about infection." He paused. "I'm still worried about it."

Michelle reached up and touched his lips. "Stop talking."

He looked taken aback for a moment, then smiled. "Sorry about that."

"What's your plan?"

The team experimented on the luminescent material, using everything from brute strength to tools to Cale's powers. They already knew it was soft enough to mark. With judicious use of Maia's multitool and Burleigh's axe, they removed a long section of the material from the wall in one piece. Harry rested while they worked, only moving enough to reinforce the ice holding the liquid metal in place as it sloshed back and forth. It hadn't formed itself into anything effective at digging into the ice, suggesting that perhaps Tlalit or whatever intelligence was controlling the spiders couldn't reach them to sufficiently direct them. They determined that the material did act exactly like a fiber optic line, shining Cale's light through it unimpeded, even when the material was bent sharply. If it would carry light, even around corners, it should carry other sorts of radiation . . .

. . . Like radio waves.

As they'd worked, Maia happened to look toward the door and saw Tlalit standing behind the mass of ice, watching them work. His face was impassive behind his bushy hair and beard, and his arms were crossed. It was hard to tell because of the distortion from the ice, but she thought things were moving beneath his flesh. It creeped her out to the point that she asked Harry if he could scoop up a layer of dust and broken rock from the permafrost and cement it into some more ice so she wouldn't be able to see Tlalit clearly. Harry agreed, especially because he didn't want the hybrid watching their efforts and possibly figure out a way to stop them.

Tanya was all for Harry using the ice to crush Tlalit into pulp, but he shook his head. "We don't know he's not human, and he probably could have killed us immediately but he didn't."

"That is because he wants to make us like Sara!" Tanya hissed. "If I can't kill him, I will kill myself before I let myself become . . . violated."

"I'm not a murderer, Tanya," Harry said softly.

"I'm not either," Burleigh said, "but this is survival we're talkin' about here."

"Nobody is murdering anyone," Cale said. "Not while there's a chance of making peace."

Tanya spun on her heel and stalked across the room. Maia started to follow her but she caught Burleigh's eye and he shook his head almost imperceptibly. She understood Tanya probably needed a few minutes to calm herself down. Still, Maia understood how her Russian friend felt. The connotations of the word *violated* carried a lot of dread-inducing weight.

Using Maia's multitool, Cale had carefully opened their one undamaged radio from Sara's pack and spliced in wiring from all of their broken ones. Harry iced the stripped wires into place around the crystal at the top of the room and handed the radio to Michelle. "Try to broadcast through the radio and the wires. Hopefully the material running throughout this base will carry the signal until it reaches the surface."

"That's your plan? That's the best you've got?" Michelle snorted.

Harry shrugged. "The other option is for me to make all this ice into a giant corkscrew and see if I can tunnel us out of here before we run out of air, or I give myself a stroke."

"You could do that?" Maia asked.

"Give myself a stroke? I have no idea, but I'm exhausted. I don't know what kind of harm I could do to myself if I push too far."

"If we can't get a radio response, we'll have to try it," Cale said. "Hopefully we aren't too deep below the surface."

"That's a pretty big hope. Permafrost is over six hundred meters deep at Prudhoe Bay. I don't know if I could tunnel through it faster than a meter a minute. Do the math, boss." Harry looked even more exhausted just thinking about it.

"Maybe it won't come to that," Cale said.

Tanya snorted. Maia hadn't even noticed when she rejoined the group. "Why would we have good luck?"

Burleigh chuckled. "That's the spirit."

Michelle closed her eyes in concentration, clenching her hands on the radio.

"Do you hear anything?" Harry asked.

Michelle cracked open one eye. "Not yet. Maybe you could shut up for a minute?"

"Oh, right. Sorry again."

Burleigh covered his mouth with the back of his hand so he wouldn't laugh aloud, but the humor in his eyes nearly made Maia burst out laughing as well. She had to look away from him so she wouldn't lose it. Even so, her sides quaked with barely restrained laughter. It had to be a stress response, right? There wasn't anything funny about their situation.

Seconds turned into minutes, and minutes crawled by with the slowness of an Arctic glacier as sweat beaded on Michelle's forehead. Burleigh used the hem of his shirt to blot it away. Maia had to stand up and walk around; the stress was making it hard for her to sit still. She went over to check on the *Atlanta Nights* crew. They were all still unconscious. The rest of the team had debated whether it would be safer for them to lie on their backs or their stomachs. Harry had won that argument, saying their backs would be most tender due to the needles. In the unpleasant event any of them vomited, it would be safer for them to be on their stomachs.

Their bodies were warm to the touch, and pulses still fluttered in their necks, although at what Maia thought was an unnaturally slow rate. She wondered if they would survive what had happened to them, or if it could be reversed.

She turned her attention to the icy tank holding the liquid metal. It still sloshed back and forth regularly, like it was agitated. When she approached it, it seemed to tense up, and solidified into a solid column of metal. Irregularities moved across its surface. She wondered if it was trying to communicate with her or had some other motive. Maybe it recognized her. Some portion of it had probably helped to carry her all the way from the lifeboat wreck. Or maybe it simply saw her as a hybrid like Tlalit and was trying to obtain new orders.

Thinking of Tlalit made her turn toward the room's exit. Harry's debris barrier remained in place, but she could still see through it, and Tlalit was gone. His absence made her blood run cold. He'd been staring at them for a long time, and his disappearance meant he'd come to some sort of decision on his next course of action. Whatever it was, it couldn't be good.

She went over to Cale. "Tlalit is gone," she said quietly.

"I know," Cale said. "He's been gone for some time. I didn't see when he left."

"What do you think he's up to?"

"I have no idea, but I'm sure it's bad for us. We've done a lot of damage to his operation. I suspect that they were unprepared for the possibility of parahumans."

"Who could blame them, yeah?"

"Maia, I want you to know that I'm extremely proud of you and the way you've handled yourself during this call-out. You're showing a lot of composure. I know this year is an internship year for you, but I'm recommending you for immediate membership once we get back. You'll probably never be tested in a hotter fire than this, and you've performed at an exceptional level."

Maia's mouth dropped open but she couldn't find any words. She'd spent most of her life being told she wasn't good enough even to be around normal people. Now she was exceptional? How was she supposed to take that?

Cale smiled. "Just say *thank you, Midnight Sun.*"

"Uh, thank you, Midnight Sun."

"See? Exceptional performance." Cale patted her shoulder and she felt like she'd just been given a lengthy vacation at an oceanside resort with unlimited swimming privileges. She turned back to the rest of the team and realized that *she was part of that team.* For the first time in her life, she belonged somewhere.

She burst into tears. "I'm s-sorry. It's j-just that . . ."

"It's okay, Maia. It's been a hard day. When this is over, we've all earned a break."

Michelle's eyes flew open. "I heard something! Not lightning or static . . . a broadcast. I'm sending a distress call. Hang on . . ." She winced. Veins bulged at her temples and her face turned crimson. One of her hands fluttered helplessly and Burleigh grabbed it. Maia saw Michelle's knuckles whiten as she clenched her fingers around Burleigh's. She screamed like a power weightlifter going for a world record. Blood ran from her nostrils and ears. Capillaries burst across her face and in her eyes. She arched her back, despite her broken ribs, every muscle in her body contracting like she was having a seizure, then slumped down into unconsciousness.

"Jesus Christ!" Burleigh cried, and reached a hand down to check the pulse against the side of her neck.

"She damn near just killed herself," Harry said, his voice hoarse. "Her heart feels like she just ran a marathon. Blood pressure is spiking. I'm sedating her." He yanked an injector from his first aid kit, pulled the safety cap from it with his teeth, then jammed the injector home into her thigh. "Come on, girl. Stabilize."

The radio crackled.

Chapter Twenty-One

*From Maia's playlist: "Voices in the Sky" - *The Moody Blues*

"Just Cause Arctic Circle, this is the Preserve. We have received your mayday transmission. Please respond, over." The voice was feminine and authoritative.

Cale sprang for the radio, for once moving even faster than Tanya. "Preserve, this is Just Cause Arctic Circle. Mayday, mayday, mayday. Repeat, this is Just Cause Arctic Circle. We are receiving you, over."

A few seconds of silence passed before the voice on the radio spoke again. "Just Cause Arctic Circle, please state your location, over."

"Our exact location is unknown. Repeat, exact location unknown. Last known location was approximately one hundred forty klicks east by northeast of JCAC headquarters in the Arctic Ocean, over."

More seconds ticked by with no response from the Preserve, whatever that was. "Why are they waiting so long?" Maia whispered.

Tanya shrugged.

Cale opened his mouth to transmit again but the radio voice spoke once more. "We are isolating your location, Just Cause Arctic Circle. Please state the nature of your emergency, over."

Cale glanced at the others. "I'm going to tell them the truth. Anybody opposed to that?"

Harry looked up from where he was listening to Michelle's heart through the stethoscope and gave Cale a thumbs-up.

"Go for it, boss," Burleigh said.

Cale nodded. "Okay, here goes nothing." He pressed the *transmit* button. "We are reporting the presence of hostile extraterrestrials. Repeat, hostile extraterrestrials. We have twelve people total, and seven wounded, over."

The pause seemed interminable. "They've got to be thinking that last one over, yeah? Hostile extraterrestrials," Maia said.

"It's not as far-fetched as it might have been before the Hind attacked," Cale said.

"Stand by, Just Cause Arctic Circle. We have located you. We're sending assistance. Repeat, assistance is on the way. Stand by, over."

Maia gasped. "They found us underground—or wherever we are? How long until we get help?"

"Cale, you need to warn them," Harry said as he put away the stethoscope. "Potential biological and nanotech contamination. We can't let this stuff get out into the rest of the world."

"How can they help us?" Tanya asked.

Cale shrugged and brought the radio back up to his mouth. "Preserve, this is Just Cause Arctic Circle. Be advised there is a risk of biological and nanotech contamination. We recommend full quarantine protocols. Repeat, biological and nanotech contamination, over."

Maia felt like the pause was long enough that she could have taken a nap. "Why are they waiting so long to reply to us?"

"What's the Preserve?" Burleigh asked, but nobody had an answer for him.

"Potential contamination confirmed, Just Cause Arctic Circle. That's not going to present a problem. Stand by, over."

A new voice broke into the radio. "Hey, uh, please stand back from the radio."

Cale blinked and looked at the others. "Did he just say *stand back*?"

A cloud of blue and gold energy swirled from the radio to resolve into a man in an old-school one-piece bodysuit. It was a bright sky blue that shone even in Cale's dimmed light, with golden lines running down from the shoulders and then turning right angles toward the center of his chest but stopping part way, ending in dots with an arch over the top. He immediately fell to his hands and knees and vomited.

Cale jumped back out of the way and the others gasped or shouted in surprise at the man's sudden appearance. Tanya gagged at the sound of the man's enthusiastic puking and Maia couldn't blame her—it made her feel queasy as well.

The man accepted a hand up from Burleigh. Despite his heroic costume, he didn't have a particularly heroic build about him. His arms and legs were skinny and the costume didn't fit him well, bunching in the crotch and under the arms and stretching too tightly across an incipient paunch. "Oh God . . . what the—ugh—" He spat to one side. "What the hell are you guys using for signal amplification in here? I feel like I just got spat from a roller coaster into a meat grinder."

"Who the hell are you?" Burleigh asked in unbridled astonishment.

The man wiped his mouth with the back of his hand, then grimaced at the stain on his glove. "Name's Circuit Breaker."

"Did you just . . . transmit yourself over the radio?" Harry asked.

"Sure enough." Circuit Breaker grinned proudly.

"That's crazy. I never heard of anyone who could do that."

"I'm pretty much the only one, as far as I know." Circuit Breaker looked around the room. "Where the hell are we, anyway? Somewhere underground, right?"

"Your guess is as good as ours," Cale said. "We don't know where *here* is. We were brought here as prisoners."

"And what—no, we can figure that all out later." Circuit Breaker counted all the people in the room. "Twelve. Goddamn, you weren't kidding. This is going to be a hell of a thing. Okay, here's what's going to happen. I need you all to be in physical contact with each other, including the unconscious and wounded. I can't do this without a single point of contact or somebody gets left behind." He paused. "How about that guy?"

Maia and the others turned to look where he was pointing. The liquid metal behind Harry's ice barrier had formed itself into a grotesquely overmuscled humanoid figure and as they watched, it started pummeling the ice with its fists, over and over, making the ice shiver with every blow.

"That's the bad guy," Cale said. "If you can get us out of here, now's the time."

"Okay, get yourselves ready. Soon as you're all touching, we're out of here. Trip is going to take a couple of seconds. Your senses will be completely blanked out, but you'll be conscious and you won't be able to breathe, move, or speak. It's a little, uh, scary . . . even if you're expecting it." Circuit Breaker turned his attention to a unit strapped to his forearm and began typing in information on a built-in keyboard.

The five heroes of Just Cause Arctic Circle carefully placed each unconscious *Atlanta Nights*' crewman's hand on the chest of the man next to him. Harry took Michelle's hand; Tanya took his and Maia's. Burleigh took Maia's other hand, then grabbed onto Cale, who touched the last crewman in the line. "Okay, we're set," he said.

Just as he spoke, Harry's ice wall shattered under the liquid metal's onslaught and it flowed outward like an angry wave toward them.

Circuit Breaker reached out to take Cale's wrist and the entire world went away.

* * *

Even though Maia could hold her breath for half an hour at a time, the two seconds of pure nothingness had her gasping for air as she fell to the floor, completely disoriented by what she assumed was teleportation. Her fall was strangely slow, and her reflexive motion to catch herself sent her bouncing across the gray metallic surface like a beach ball. She came to a stop and spread out her hands and feet as if she was hugging the ground. She raised her head enough to look around, not quite understanding what had happened.

She, the rest of Just Cause Arctic Circle, and the *Atlanta Nights* crewmen were in a large rectangular room made of smooth metal with rounded corners. Panels in the roof provided cool blue-white light, while a pair of red dome lights on opposite walls rotated in a silent warning or alert. As she watched, Circuit Breaker pushed several buttons on a control panel next to him. The warning lights turned off. "Everybody here?"

The other members of JCAC were staggering, as off-balance as Maia had been. Poor Tanya's motion sickness came on full force and she was retching, hunched over in a ball of misery. "Where is *here*?" Cale asked.

"The Preserve," said a new voice, matching the one that had originally contacted them over the radio. "Welcome."

Maia turned to see a woman regarding them from across the room. She wore a suit of tight-fitting metallic blue armor with red and gold highlights. Her brown hair hung around her face and she smiled down at them.

"Hey, I know you," Burleigh said. "Aren't you Penny Lane? I thought you were dead."

Harry shook his head. "No, I remember. She resigned from Just Cause, or something, after fighting the Hind."

Penny smiled. "*Something* is pretty accurate. I found an avocation that suits me a little better than being JCNY's resident sniper."

"What's that?" Cale asked.

"Protecting the Earth."

"What, like, all of it?" Harry asked. "By yourself?"

"Not entirely. I've got a team. You've already met Benjie." Circuit Breaker waved and grinned. "You'll meet the others shortly. They're preparing the operating theater to receive your wounded. Especially those six naked men who are giving off some really . . . *odd* readings."

Maia got to her feet, feeling strangely bouncy. "Hey, uh, where are we? In the world, I mean."

Penny waved a hand and previously hidden shutters opened along one wall to show a rocky gray landscape overlooking a cratered surface, and beyond that a field of inky blackness peppered by a thousand unblinking stars. Just on the horizon, almost entirely obscured but for a few valleys, they saw a brilliant blue and white arc that could only be one thing.

"Oh, shit," Maia said. "We're on the Moon, yeah?"

Penny laughed. "You know, I said exactly the same thing my first time here." She looked out over the barren landscape. "It's still amazing."

Chapter Twenty-Two

From Maia's playlist: "Walking on the Moon" - <u>The Police</u>

Penny introduced the JCAC heroes to her . . . well, Maia wasn't quite sure what to call them. *Coworkers* didn't seem right, as Penny was clearly in charge of the group. *Employees* didn't fit either. They were a team, but a team with far more independence and lenience than would have been permitted in any kind of official capacity. They were not associated with the Parahuman Resources Administration in any way. In fact, Penny said, she'd rather that the JCAC heroes kept the information about the Preserve to themselves.

"The last thing I need is some gung ho military or government types deciding that this location is more important strategically to them than it is to me. I'd rather not have to defend myself against humans. That's not why I'm here."

"Why are you here?" Cale asked. "You said you're protecting the Earth, but from what? And how? And how does the Hind fit in?" He nodded toward the alien standing quietly behind Penny like a cross between a centaur and a lion. All the pictures Maia had ever seen of the alien invaders showed them wearing samurai-like battle armor and carrying axes and oversized laser rifles. This one wore no armor and carried no weapon. He had a satchel slung over one shoulder but besides that, he was naked but for his thick coat of tawny fur.

"Garragh is a friend," Penny said. "His is a complicated story. For now, let's just say that he's a defector and call it good. "I trust him without reservation, and even if you don't because of what he is, you can be assured that you are as safe around him as you are around me."

"Are we safe around you?" Tanya asked.

"You are." A familiar tall, slender black man walked into the lounge, carrying a tray of sandwiches. It was Mustang Sally's beau and the father of her children, March Washington. "Hello, Maia," he said with a sheepish smile.

"Wow, it's you," Maia said. "I mean, your kids said you were going to the Moon. I didn't think they meant it literally, yeah?"

March laughed. "They're not v-very good at keeping secrets. Lucky for me, n-nobody takes toddlers seriously."

"So Mustang Sally knows about this place?"

"Of course. She visits on th-the weekends sometimes. Or I visit her."

"You guys must have unreal frequent flyer miles," Harry said. "Or do you all take the Circuit Breaker Express?"

"Sometimes," Penny said. "But not too often. It's hard for him to travel to and from here with a lot of baggage. Or passengers," she added as if an afterthought. "We've got other means of transportation here as well."

"You got a spaceship?" Burleigh asked. "Are we gonna get to ride in it?"

"Maybe. If you ask nicely." Penny smiled. "Of course you are. That's how I'm taking you back home." Her smile vanished. "But first things first." She clasped her hands behind her back. "When the Hind attacked seven years ago, we learned we were officially not the only intelligent life in the Universe. And we learned we weren't even the frontrunners. There is always the possibility the Hind will come back, and if so, someone needs to be ready for them. Harlan Washington built this place years ago as his own private refuge. He passed it to me before his death and I've expanded it. I have sensors that reach all the way to the edges of the Solar System. If something—or some*one*—comes calling, I'll have plenty of warning and I'll know if I need to . . . address it."

The Hind nodded in a very human gesture. Maia kept shooting curious glances his way. She would have said it was the first time she'd ever seen an alien if it hadn't been for the events beneath the Arctic ice.

"You and your team?" Harry asked, swirling his hot chocolate around his mug and watching it jiggle in the lower lunar gravity.

"Me and whomever I require. I have a lot of contacts on the world below, even though I spend most of my time watching the stars." She smiled. "The rest of the folks here help tend to more earthly events. You've already met Benjie, of course. He's a former member of a black ops group that is part of the Central Intelligence Agency. He zapped himself away after his last mission and technically he's a fugitive, but it's not like anybody could contain him. Not even in Deep Six."

A boy several years younger than Maia bounced into the room, making the most of the gravity. He bopped over to a table, snagged a cookie, then flung himself onto a couch and stared unabashedly at the JCAC heroes. Penny smiled. "This bundle of energy is my son, Avery. He's dying to ask you all a bunch of questions." She gave him a severe look. "Avery, we have guests. Use your words."

"Sorry, mom," he said, not sounding the least bit apologetic. "Why don't you give them nanocomms like we have?"

"Because not everybody needs one, Avery. Your father doesn't have one. How do you communicate with him?"

Avery sniffed. "I try not to. He's boring." He brightened up. "Hey, do you guys want to see the genome bank?"

"What's that?" Burleigh asked. He'd been slowly but steadily demolishing a plate of sandwiches along with Maia, who had finally realized how hungry she was and gave in to her body's demands.

"The Preserve is more than just a defensive outpost," Penny said. "I have been slowly building a library of genomes for as many Earth species as I can. Like the seed bank in Norway, but much more comprehensive. It's a losing battle, of course. There are over eight million species on the Earth at last count, and my team is small, but knowing about spacefaring civilizations and the risk of global catastrophe has convinced me more than ever that we cannot put all our eggs into one basket. If the Earth were to dissolve into gray goo tomorrow, I would have more than one million genetic samples representing over two hundred thousand species stored here in a secure vault deep under the surface. It's enough biodiversity to start several complex biomes in a variety of settings."

Tanya asked, "Are you going to colonize another world?"

Penny laughed. "Only if they have New York-style pizza."

Another woman, quite a bit older than Penny or March entered the room. She was dark-skinned, with her gray hair cut close to her scalp. She wore what looked like a cross between a kimono and a bathrobe over some simple, comfortable clothing. "Hello, everyone," she said. "I'm Juliet. I've been monitoring the progress of your teammate and your civilian rescues. First, the good news. Your friend Simulcast is recovering. We've used our own nanotech here to help repair her damaged ribs and to seal the puncture to her lung. The prognosis is excellent and after a couple days' rest, she should be as good as new."

"You can heal people that quickly?" Harry asked.

"When called upon to do so. Injuries like Simulcast sustained are not difficult to repair with Washington's nanotech. The damage done by the

Arctic aliens to the civilians with you is another story." She looked dismayed. "Their cells have been attacked at nearly an atomic level. The infection is spreading and not only can we not contain it, we're at risk for contaminating our own nanotech stockpiles. I've got all six men in isolation, separated from the rest of the Preserve by a vacuum gap. I can't promise they will survive. I have never seen anything like it."

"If anyone can figure it out, Juliet, it'll be you," Penny said.

"I still think you need to get Dr. Devereaux's team in Paris involved," Juliet replied. "They're better set up for this kind of thing. I know you've still got healers in your extended Just Cause contacts. Surely you can risk bringing one of them up here."

Penny turned back to the JCAC heroes. "We're still discussing options, obviously. It's a balance of security of the Preserve against the survival of those civilians you brought with you. We don't want to lose them, but we can't afford to risk compromising the Preserve either. March is working on finding a way to reprogram the alien nanotech, but it's complicated when you have no common frame of reference. It's like trying to teach a dolphin to ride a bicycle."

Maia laughed. "Next time I go swimming with them, I'm going to give that a try, yeah?"

"Shoot video," Avery said. "It'll go viral."

"Avery . . ." Penny had that tone that all mothers seemed to get when they were *done* with their children. "Don't you have homework to do?"

He shrugged. "Finished it."

"Cleaning?"

"Nah, this is more interesting."

Penny frowned. "All right, you can stay, but any more comments from the peanut gallery and I'm sending you out to sweep the crater."

Avery rolled his eyes but nodded. Apparently the threat didn't carry as much weight as the intent behind it.

Penny turned back to the JCAC heroes. "I'm sorry about that."

Cale shook his head. "No apologies necessary. We're just glad to be here and not, you know, dying from alien nanotech contaminating our DNA."

"Here's the problem we're having," Juliet said. "The alien genome is insidious stuff. I'm having a hell of a time isolating it from human DNA. It's very good at integrating itself. What I really need is an uncontaminated sample of the source material so I can try to reverse engineer a viral cure."

Maia gasped. "Oh! I have something!"

Penny narrowed her eyes. "Where?"

Maia reached into her pack and withdrew the robotic spider leg, curled up into a knot once more. "This is from that liquid metal that the spiders were made of, yeah?"

"Avery, Garragh, go with Juliet to the scanner room *right now*," Penny said in a voice that brooked no argument.

Avery's eyes widened at his mother's tone and he jumped off the couch, practically running across the room after Juliet, who was a dozen steps ahead of him. Garragh sprang over couches, his heavy-gravity muscles propelling him like a furry missile. As soon as the three of them had left the room, every door slammed shut, sealing all of the JCAC heroes into the room with Penny.

"You brought alien technology here and didn't tell me?" Penny's frosty tone gave Maia the chills.

"I—I didn't remember I had it," Maia stammered. "I'm sorry!" Burleigh stepped over to stand beside her like a bodyguard.

Penny pinched the bridge of her nose. "No, I'm sorry. I should have done more than a cursory scan on you all. I don't believe any of you are contaminated, but I need to be sure. I didn't mean to yell. I tend to take my job seriously." She touched all her fingertips together, then spread them apart as if she was holding the sides of an invisible frame. A previously unseen membrane stretched between her fingers. It was translucent, with data streaming across it. She viewed each JCAC hero in turn through the membrane, apparently scanning them with some sort of personal nanotechnology.

"You okay, kid?" Burleigh asked Maia, placing a heavy, comforting hand upon her shoulder.

"Yeah," she said softly. "I've been yelled at before."

"I'm sorry about that."

"It's not your fault, Burleigh."

"It's not yours either, kid. Don't forget that."

"Looks like you're clear enough that I don't have to isolate you," Penny said. "However, I'm going to have Juliet scan each of you in-depth. It won't be intrusive, but it will be time-consuming. I hope none of you have anywhere to be."

"Is that Arctic cyclone still hammering the top of the world?" Cale asked. "We'd probably be hunkered down under cover waiting for it to wrap up if it's not done yet."

"It's still going," Penny said after a moment, perhaps checking some hidden data source. "Wind speed is down to sixty-eight knots. That's Category One. Give it a few more hours and I think it'll just be windy and not particularly dangerous. Your weather up there is weird."

Harry chuckled. "Yeah, tell us about it."

"I guess we're stuck here for the time being," Cale said. "We're sorry to intrude."

"Not at all," Penny said. "On the contrary, I'm very glad you turned up. It's much better to find out about something like this now before it turns into the kind of problem I can't deal with on a small scale." She held out a hand to Maia. "I'll take that piece of nanotech if you don't mind, Devilfish. And again, I apologize for blowing up at you."

Maia nodded and handed the rolled-up leg to Penny. "It's cool. I think it's awesome that you're up here on the Moon, watching over us like a guardian angel, yeah? I'll think of it every time I look up now." She tried a brave smile.

Penny reciprocated, which made Maia feel a lot better.

Chapter Twenty-Three

From Maia's playlist: "The Battle Rages On" - Deep Purple

Maia was the first one Penny called to get the full-body scan. She was nervous and didn't know what to expect. Penny seemed so brusque at times and Maia was afraid of offending her all over again. That fear seemed unfounded after a few minutes, as Penny made a real effort to put her at ease. "So that tech you brought is pretty interesting," Penny said as she brought Maia into another room of the Preserve. Maia had thought maybe it would be like a big MRI machine or something, but instead there was a simple ring on the floor with a matching ring on the ceiling of the room. A device ran from floor to ceiling outside the ring and looked like it was designed to move around the circle. "It's not like any nanotech I've seen. There's more data coded into these alien machines than anything we've managed. Whoever designed them was maybe thousands of years more advanced than we are, technologically speaking."

"Harry said he thought they were millions of years older, yeah?" Maia said. "There were dinosaurs in their cave."

Penny's eyes widened. "Actual, living dinosaurs?"

"No, just like specimens, with the legs and things growing out of them."

"Like what we're trying to prevent happening to your civilians?"

"Yeah, I think so. It's what happened to Sara—uh, Snowball. They had a . . . I think maybe she was a Neanderthal too. Lots of animals. Even a saber-tooth tiger."

Penny had Maia stand in the center of the floor ring while the device rotated around her, examining her from every angle. "Millions of years, then. Hmmm. I wish I was a little more scientifically minded. Juliet, pop in here, would you?"

Although Penny didn't use any kind of obvious device to call for her, Juliet arrived a minute later. "What's up? I was looking over the genetic samples we've taken."

"Apparently these aliens have been on Earth a lot longer than we have. Maia said they have contaminated dinosaur specimens. What does that tell you?"

Juliet frowned. "We're in trouble."

* * *

"Here's the thing," Penny said after she'd completed her scans of all the JCAC members and they regrouped in the lounge once more. "We'd originally thought we could remove the alien influence from your rescues' human DNA, but it looks like that may not be a possibility, and the reason is . . . upsetting. Juliet will have to explain." She smiled at her teammate. "Try to remember that I'm basically a jarhead in a supersuit and use lots of small words."

"My first thought was to use a viral nanotech plague to seek and destroy the alien genome in the human DNA. The problem is compatibility," Juliet said.

"That's a term that Tlalit used," Harry said. "He was trying to find a life form that would be *compatible* with the alien life."

"Oh, he found one, without question. The disturbing part is *why* humans are compatible," Juliet said. "Evolution. At some point, far in Earth's past, the alien genome got out. It's already in us. It's in *all of us*."

Juliet's words hit all of them like a punch to the gut. Maia felt like all her body's nerves were trying to hide in her stomach.

"You mean we're all gonna start sproutin' five legs and pincers?" Burleigh asked.

"No, not at all. What I'm saying is that humans are compatible with the alien genome because we evolved with it in our own genetic structure. Honestly, I can't isolate what makes the alien part *alien*, because it matches a large portion of human DNA. For all I know, they succeeded in their original intention to colonize the Earth," Juliet said. "And we're the end result."

"So we are all aliens?" Tanya asked.

"Yes, and no. We are our own species, of course, evolved to live on this planet. Our evolution could have been jump-started by an influx of this alien genome. On a hunch, I checked Garragh's genetic structure. Obviously, it's very different from our own, but there is an identifiable piece in common. Your aliens, whoever they were, may have seeded life around the galaxy." Juliet sipped at a steaming mug of chai. She'd mixed up a batch and offered it around to the others. Penny politely declined, as did Burleigh, but the others were glad to accept. It was the strangest drink Maia had ever tasted, all sweet and peppery and spicy at the same time, but it warmed her in a way hot chocolate never had.

"What that means is we can't just hit your aliens with a tailored plague," Penny said. "Whatever is going on in that base, it's now a risk to the rest of the world. As much as the idea of causing an extinction makes me feel ill, the risk of them getting out and infecting humanity can't be ignored. Anything we would tailor to take out the aliens could cross the species barrier to affect naturally evolved life on Earth."

"And obviously, you can't be nuking them from orbit," Harry said. "So what are we going to do?"

"I don't see any alternative," Penny said. "I'm going to go down there and sterilize that entire facility."

"You mean *we* are," Cale said. "The Arctic is our responsibility. I know you're former Just Cause, Penny, but we can't let you go in alone. It's our mess. We should help clean it up."

"It's nobody's mess," Penny said. "This alien compound was there long before any of us showed up.

It's not a Just Cause problem, it's a human problem. Don't get me wrong. You guys are great, and you're really optimized for the climate and for search and rescue work." She crossed her arms. "Me? I'm optimized for combat. Before the Hind invasion, I was a police sniper and special weapons expert. Now I've got the same fundamental tech as Destroyer had, and with my team, I've improved upon it. I'm a walking weapon of mass destruction. You know those vague, terrible parahumans that certain factions in the governments are always warning people about?"

"Yes," Cale said.

"They mean me."

The JCAC heroes had no immediate response to that. They looked at each other, or at the floor, or out the windows at the jagged gray moonscape beyond, with the pinpricks of starlight like grains of salt spilled upon black velvet.

Penny laughed. "I'm sorry. I don't mean to come across as all dramatic. I don't interact with a lot of people anymore, and sometimes I forget how. Luckily, I've got Juliet and the others to remind me that not everybody can communicate via nanotech-powered subspace transmissions."

"That sounds . . . amazing," Harry said.

"It's actually pretty mundane. The mechanism is different but it's still just having a voice chat feature enabled," Penny said. "So here's what we're going to do. I'm not going to bring all of you with me, because I don't want to have to keep track of so many bodies beyond my own. You may consider the Arctic your responsibility, but when you travel with me, you are mine. I'll take three of you, and I'll outfit you in gear to protect you from any rogue nanotech. I'll arm you appropriately. We'll go down there and sterilize that base top to bottom, and then destroy it. There might be alien nanites that survive, but it's a good bet that it would take thousands of years before they can multiply enough to be any kind of danger. I'll make sure there is enough data in my system that any future Sentinels beyond me know what to look for."

"Future Sentinels?" Maia asked.

"Naturally," Penny said. "I'll live a lot longer than a normal human, thanks to Harlan Washington's legacy, but eventually I'll be too old to keep defending an entire world. There will be others."

"But not an entire force?" Cale asked. "You could do so much good with a larger group."

"I could also do a lot of evil," Penny said. "I've come to understand that over the years. I'm very careful about who I bring into the fold. A small group can change direction quickly without being too tied up with bureaucratic inertia. If it needs to be shut down, moved, or otherwise altered, I can do it."

"How small is your group?" Tanya asked. "Have we met everyone?"

"No, of course not. Gathering genome samples takes a lot of help. Most of those working with me stay on the Earth. It's better that way. Only a few people ever get to come up here. Loose lips sink ships . . . or destroy secret bases."

"We're honored that you're trusting us," Cale said.

Penny smiled, and Maia became suspicious that maybe she wasn't trusting them all that much.

She thought maybe she knew who Juliet was, or rather, who she had been. Way back in the Eighties, before Maia had been born, there had been a long-running private superhero team in Chicago called the Lucky Seven. They'd had a psi named Juliet, as well as several other heroes who had long since retired. Penny's teammate would be about the right age as the former hero. If Maia hadn't aced her Parahuman History class her senior year, she might not have remembered that. One thing psis were typically good at was getting into non-psionicists' minds. Perhaps that was how Penny kept the Preserve secret.

On one hand, Maia understood the need for that secrecy. Tanya had spoken about how strict the Russian government was when it came to parahumans. If they knew about the Preserve, they would see it as a strategic imperative, and they would perhaps try to capture it. Likewise, the Americans would probably claim it as their own as the sole country to have set foot upon the Moon. Either way, the knowledge of its existence could touch off a war. Like, an *actual* war, Maia thought, and the feeling made her a little sick.

On the other hand, having a psi poke around in her mind to alter or even erase her memories was equally sickening. Psionicists were the rarest classification of parahumans. There hadn't been one in her graduating class, although there was a girl in the class behind her who went by the handle *Metrist*. She could psionically track objects through time and space using what she called psychic residue. It wasn't the sort of power that was likely to earn her a spot on a Just Cause roster, but she would likely be in great demand in the private sector. She was Maia's only experience with psis before meeting Juliet.

If Juliet erased her memory, she wondered if she'd even know she'd been tampered with. Probably not, she guessed, since Juliet was highly experienced and had been doing her psionic things for some fifty years or more.

"Who do you wanna take back down to the base with you?" Burleigh asked with a hopeful expression and puppy dog eyes.

Penny chuckled. "Yes, Snowcat, I'm planning to take you. I'd also like to take Devilfish, if that's all right, Midnight Sun."

Maia's heart skipped a beat. She did want to go help, partly out of a sense of duty and partly because she simply wanted to see what Penny could do. Despite that, the idea was nerve-wracking, and if Cale overrode Penny, she'd be disappointed, but only a little. She had never thought she could say the Moon felt like a safe place, but compared to the Arctic alien base . . .

"Maia, if you want to go with Burleigh, you can," Cale said. "You've proven yourself a hundred times over, as far as I'm concerned."

"I do not wish to go." Tanya shivered as if someone had walked across her grave. "I will stay with Michelle."

Penny nodded. "I'm sure she will appreciate having friends and teammates with her. Midnight Sun, I hope you don't take it personally that I would prefer you stay here."

Cale bowed his head. "I suspected that might be the case. I know I'm not particularly useful in a combat situation."

"Don't sell yourself short. Leadership is important in times of stress, and you kept this team together and kept them all alive. That's a real accomplishment." Penny smiled. "However, I feel like Igloo would be the most useful addition to the team when it comes to sealing up the base."

Harry nodded. "Yeah, we already talked about that. It's too bad Sara didn't make it. She could have done a lot more than I can."

"Juliet will be able to help with that," Penny said. She stood from the table and motioned to the door. "Let's prepare to leave. The longer we leave that base unattended, the more likely it is something will happen that we don't want."

Chapter Twenty-Four

From Maia's playlist: "The Killing Moon"
- Echo and the Bunnymen

Maia felt like a badass right out of a Hollywood movie. It was a weird but empowering feeling. Penny took her, Burleigh, and Harry to the nanotech lab where they were wrapped in a strange material that looked and clung like plastic wrap but breathed as easily and comfortably as if they were wearing well-worn cotton t-shirts. Even though the suits covered their heads and faces, none of the heroes felt claustrophobic or strangled, since they could breathe normally. Penny explained that the nanites that formed the basis for their suits worked like revolving doors, passing air molecules from the outside of the suits to the inside, and vice versa for waste gases and excess humidity.

"They'll stop any foreign nanotech or alien contaminants from reaching your body simply by locking the doors. Sometimes the oldest tech is the best." Penny grinned. "I'm no engineer and even I understand that much."

"What if something gets through the suit?" Harry asked. "You can't plan for everything."

"The suit will let me know, and we'll get you back up to the lab for cleansing."

"Cleansing," Burleigh repeated. "Sounds . . . unpleasant."

Penny didn't address that. Instead, she brought out some weapons from her armory.

"You have an armory?" Harry asked. "I got the sense this was a much more peace-oriented kind of facility."

"It's for defense of the Earth," Penny said. "And sometimes the best defense is a proactive offense." She passed each of the heroes a rifle. "These are . . . well, you might as well call them lightning guns. They issue a directed electromagnetic pulse. It's configured for the wavelength that will affect the alien tech. Point and shoot. It shouldn't affect my own nanotech, but . . ." She winked. "Let's not find out."

"What's the plan, then?" Harry asked.

"You three keep the nanotech off me while I track down and destroy the power and data core of the facility. Once that's done, we fill the entire base with ocean water and then Harry seals it with the biggest glacier he can. It might not be the perfect solution, but it will last for thousands or even millions of years if we get lucky."

"What if it doesn't?" Maia looked at the rifle in her hands uncertainly. She'd never fired a weapon and didn't know if she even could.

"Then we'll address it at that time." Penny grinned. "Who wants to go for a ride in my spaceship?"

* * *

The spaceship looked more like a large van than something out of a summer science fiction blockbuster. It could carry up to ten passengers with March and Penny at the controls. Maia, Burleigh, Harry, and Benjie rode in the passenger compartment. The interior of the ship was practical, lined with a dark, dirt-hiding carpet. Each passenger seat had some minor amenities like a tray table, a cup holder, and a video screen with headphones. It was all so ridiculously mundane that Maia half expected March to come through the cabin with half-size cans of soda and bags of flavorless nuts.

The ship was nearly silent in its operation, which spoke either of exceptional insulation or else the engines operated without noise. Either way, she'd been on passenger jets that were far noisier.

The Earth drew closer and closer until it filled the cockpit windows. "How long does it take to get there?" Maia asked.

Burleigh chuckled. "Ma, are we there yet?"

"A few hours." Penny turned back to look at her passengers. "This ship is quite a bit faster than the Apollo missions. If I was flying direct, I could do it in two hours, but it takes a lot of power and it's . . . uncomfortable. Nobody could do it who wasn't enhanced by nanotech. There's plenty of entertainment and news available on your screens to keep you busy if you like."

"How's the hurricane?" Harry asked.

"Your cyclone? It's basically done. The wind's still blowing and the seas are rough, but not like they were twelve hours ago. It sounds like they'll start reopening the rigs in about ten hours."

"Is anyone, you know, asking about us?" Maia asked. "I mean, it's no secret we flew into the storm to rescue the *Atlanta Nights* crew, yeah?"

Penny nodded. "Before we left, I had Cale send a message to JCAC Command. As far as they know, you're all holed up in a safe location until the storm passes and you'll call for a pickup once the weather is safe. By that time, I hope we'll be done clearing that base and nobody will be the wiser."

"Why didn't you just erase our memories and go do all this yourself?" Harry asked. Maia was glad he brought up the same thoughts she'd been having. She didn't understand that herself. If Penny was so careful to keep the Preserve a secret, why was she allowing such a security breach in the surviving members of JCAC?

"Couple of reasons," Penny said. "First of all, I've got a good sense of who can keep quiet and who can't. You don't spend as many years in law enforcement as I did without learning to read people. You guys aren't going to put me in your reports to the PRA, and you're not going to sell my story to the first tabloid who shakes a hundred grand at you."

Harry raised his hand. "Don't underestimate the power of human greed."

"Also, Juliet may have put psionic blocks in place in your minds as an insurance policy. You can talk about me and Preserve as much as you like with each other, but if you think about bringing it up to someone outside of your team, you're going to find it very difficult to put into words."

Burleigh gasped. "You messed with our minds?"

"Yes I did. This is bigger than you, Snowcat. It's bigger than all of you."

"I'm glad you didn't take it all away, yeah?" Maia looked out the porthole at the gleaming curve of the Earth, oceans sparkling blue and brilliant white clouds swirling over the Arctic. "I'd hate to forget this."

"I thought I'd get tired of it," Penny said. "But I haven't yet." She sat in silence for a minute, taking in the beautiful vista of the Earth like she was regarding a rare jewel. In a way, Maia supposed, she was. When Penny spoke again, her voice was softer, more subdued. "The other reason I need you along is that no matter how much of a badass I think I am, unexpected things happen with alarming regularity. It's better to be overprepared than underprepared. When that stuff happens today, it's better that I have a few more pairs of eyes, hands, and weapons than just my own."

"Still don't like that you were muckin' about in my brain," Burleigh grumbled.

"We can make it so you don't know we did. I feel like full disclosure is better for building trust." Penny smiled and turned back to the controls.

"Sounds like that tech isn't the only thing she got from Destroyer," Burleigh said. "I heard he was a sociopath."

"I heard he saved a lot of lives when he took out the Hind fleet, yeah?" Maia said. "Maybe being in charge of the entire world is more stressful than we think."

Harry chuckled. "Nothing like a little mindless violence to ward off stress."

* * *

Coming in through the atmosphere was an experience Maia wasn't sure she'd ever want to repeat. The descent from space was fast and enshrouded the ship in a wreath of superheated air, even though Penny said the small vessel had adequate shielding to bully its way right through the atmosphere under full power. If they were coming down over a heavily populated area, they might be the subject of numerous YouTube videos about meteorites—or UFOs, depending upon the scientific bent of those doing the posting. Coming in over the Arctic sea in the wake of a hurricane, it was unlikely that anyone would see the white heat streak in the sky.

Inside the cabin, the occupants were buffeted and jostled like they were on the world's highest roller coaster. Maia was glad Tanya hadn't come along, for the motion would have left her in a helpless puddle of vomit.

"Benjie, I need you now, please," Penny called back over her shoulder as the ship leveled out its flight over a broad ice plain.

Circuit Breaker unstrapped himself and moved forward to stand between Penny and March. "Ready."

"All r-receivers on," March said. "Stand b-by."

Circuit Breaker placed his hands on the cockpit walls like he was bracing himself. Electricity danced around his palms.

"Anything?" Penny asked after a couple of seconds.

Benjie snorted. "Who do you think I am, Kali? No, nothing yet."

"What's he doin'?" Burleigh asked.

"He's trying to concentrate," Benjie retorted. "And it's not as easy as it looks, especially with everyone yapping in my ears." He paused. "I don't think it's here. Head twenty klicks northwest. I think it's closer to the shore."

A few minutes passed as the strangely silent ship flew low over the ice field, shuddering as gusts from the dissipating storm swirled around beneath the clouds. A squall of sleet and rain splattered against the canopy, obscuring their forward vision until March touched a control that cleared the windscreen as easily as if wipers had swept over it.

"There!" Benjie said. "Half a klick, ten o'clock from our current heading." The ship angled gradually left, slowing its forward velocity until it was barely inching forward. "Almost there . . . almost there . . . stop!"

"March, how far are we from the shore?"

"Only th-thirty meters."

"Think you can carve a new channel out?"

"Yes."

"Make sure it's deep enough to fill. I don't want a few dozen gallons in that place. I want the entire ocean."

March shot her a look, unsmiling, eyes narrowed, that Maia interpreted as him not needing to be told how to do his job.

Penny must have interpreted it the same way, and she nodded. "Good enough." She slipped out of her seat to confront the others. "So here's how this is going to happen. We're all going down at once, following the signal to your old radio. Then Benjie is going to pop back up here and wait for the extraction call. With me down there, he can find us wherever we are, so long as we're all together. We go down, fight our way to the core, and do enough damage so this place can't hybridize any more people."

"Or animals," Maia said.

Penny laughed. "Or animals, thank you."

"You think they know we're coming?" Harry asked.

"They'd be fools not to. How much resistance can we expect?"

Harry shrugged. "Your guess is as good as mine. I don't know how much liquid metal they've got or if there are other hybrids able to fight. Sara gave us a tough time and it was just her. The liquid metal overwhelmed all of us. Admittedly, we're not the best combat team in Just Cause."

"You survived, you rescued the hostages. You've got nothing to be ashamed of. He who fights and runs away lives to come back with the Sentinel in tow." Blue armor seemed to flow right out of Penny's skin, wrapping her in its loving embrace. The armor kept growing and expanding as weapons appeared from the smooth surface. Wrist blasters formed, their lenses glowing with barely contained energy. A long tube sprouted from Penny's back to swivel forward on one shoulder. Secondary arms emerged beneath her natural arms, each bearing what looked like a small machine gun.

"You look like . . . a tank on legs, yeah?" Maia said.

Penny—or maybe now was the time to refer to her as the Sentinel—nodded. "Let's go say hello."

Chapter Twenty-Five

From Maia's playlist: "War Pigs" - <u>Black Sabbath</u>

Someone in the base had moved the radio that the Just Cause Arctic Circle team had left behind. When they'd departed, the radio had been in the same room where the base had been trying to turn humans into alien hybrids. When Maia and the others emerged from the radio, they were in a large dodecahedral room, featureless but for a single entrance on the lower plane of one wall. It was plugged shut with a mass of metal, possibly liquid but solidified in its current state. The familiar luminescent minerals wove through the walls, giving the room a sickly blue-white appearance like a monitor with the brightness turned up too far.

The radio lay in the middle of the room, and the team appeared around it like they were worshipers of some rare totem. Penny's weapons immediately swiveled to cover as many directions as possible, but found no targets. The motion of Penny's shoulder cannon reminded Maia that she had a rifle, and she raised it tentatively, not really knowing what she was supposed to do with it. The barrel shook and she realized she was terrified. What was she doing, trying to be some kind of space marine fighting aliens? All she wanted was to go dive into the ocean and hide in its depths until she *had* to surface long enough to breathe before disappearing again.

Benjie vanished immediately, sucked into the radio as he transmitted himself back to the waiting ship somewhere overhead.

Burleigh was beside her, his own rifle held at high point. He seemed as ill at ease with it as Maia was with hers. He kept reaching back to brush his fingers against his axe head, as if to reassure himself the weapon hadn't gone anywhere in the past few seconds. He noticed Maia's discomfiture and gently raised the barrel of her rifle until, like his, it was pointing up toward the ceiling. "Easy, kid. Remember why we're here. We're the backup." He nodded toward Penny. "She's the main force."

Harry had his hands in the air, trying to sense the ice beyond the walls. He shook his head. "Nothing. Either we're too far from the permafrost or these walls are too thick." He looked around the room. "So this looks like a dead end. What do you think they're waiting for?"

"Probably takes a few minutes to run out here on those goofy-ass five legs," Burleigh said.

"I've got a fix on where we need to go," Penny said. "But it looks like we're going to have company. I've got multiple inbound signals." She paused. "Um, it's kind of a lot." Her shoulder cannon swiveled down to face the door and she raised all four of her arms to point at it. "It's *really* a lot."

"They may still try to capture us alive, to infect us," Harry said. "That's the one thing we have going for us."

Energy crackled around the mouth of Penny's cannon. "That's not the only thing you have. Watch your corners. They may try to get at you from behind or above. Here they come."

Maia didn't even have time for Penny's terrifying statement to sink in as the metal door seemed to erupt inward in a wave of dozens or hundreds of the liquid metal spiders.

Penny opened up with all her weapons, sounding like an entire battalion going to war in the confined space of the room. Her wrist blasters cut a swath of destruction through the attacking spiders. Her secondary guns chattered until the barrels glowed red hot. Bullets chewed into spiders, sending them flying back as if they were caught in a gale. As Penny kept firing, her feet slowly sank into the floor. Perhaps instead of storing ammunition, her armor drew bullet material from the ground itself, Maia thought, transfixed by the vision of the blue-armored warrior.

Harry crouched behind Penny, clenching and opening his hands as if he could make his powers work without an ice source.

Then Penny fired her cannon into the midst of the incoming wave and it was like throwing a grenade into a lake. Liquid metal splashed in all directions, reforming itself in a second and suddenly there were spiders all around them. "Maia, fight!" Burleigh shouted over the thunderous din of Penny's weapons.

Maia remembered her rifle just in time as a clawed liquid metal hand as big as she was lunged at her from the wall. She screamed and fired the rifle at it. Arcing electricity blasted forth from the rifle's mouth. Half the hand before her collapsed into sparkling dust in a great swirling cloud while the rest recoiled, trying to reform itself although half of it was missing.

More lightning flared as Burleigh and Harry opened up with their rifles. Harry swept his along the back wall as more spiders skittered around the edges of the room, trying to encapsulate them from behind. Burleigh snapped off shots to Penny's left to keep it clear, while Maia fired to the right again and again. Every time she pulled the trigger, metal shattered apart into glitter until the entire room was awash in it. If not for the nanotech suits Penny had given her and Burleigh, they'd be breathing those particles with who knew what kinds of horrible side effects.

Then Maia pulled the trigger and nothing happened. Burleigh's rifle likewise seemed to have lost its juice. He threw it aside and pulled his axe from its hooks on his back. "Come on!" he roared, and swung it, splattering a metal spider against the far wall like he was knocking a fastball into the second level.

A half dozen spiders dropped from the ceiling to land upon Penny, stretching their tendrils around to try to envelop her upper torso. She screamed obscenities as the nanites of her armor and the spiders did battle with one another, looking for all the world like different shades of paint flowing and roiling over each other.

"Maia, help Sentinel!" Harry shouted.

"I think I'm empty," Maia said

"Somebody shoot me!" Penny screamed. Harry didn't hesitate. He squeezed off two shots directly at the liquid metal streaming and flowing over Penny's torso. The silvery liquid burst into fragments, as did a large chunk of Penny's own nanotech, leaving behind only a tight-fitting black bodysuit beneath. "Oh, goddammit."

"That was my last shot," Harry said. "We're in trouble."

Penny's armor redistributed itself around her body, peeling away from her legs and absorbing the secondary weapon arms back into itself so it could strengthen the protection around her torso and head and repair the structural support that had held the shoulder cannon. Burleigh swung his axe again and again, but it felt to Maia just like their futile battle at the lifeboat. They were going to be overwhelmed and there didn't seem to be anything they could—

"Maia!" Penny shouted, and the shoulder cannon swung around to point almost directly at her. "Duck!"

Maia threw herself to the floor, sending a cloud of nanite dust into the air.

The cannon spat a shell of some kind into the wall, sending shrapnel and debris flying over Maia's head. Her ears rang from the impact. Beyond the rock wall of the room lay a dirty, gravelly mass of ice.

Harry crowed in triumph and a massive column of ice erupted from the hole. "There's a whole goddamn *glacier* here," he said, sweeping the ice into a clawed wedge to push away all the spiders. In spite of losing their effective weapons and the damage to Penny's armor, they *had* managed a lot of damage against the alien nanotech. They were ankle-deep in dead nanites and the air was so full of their disabled corpses that it was like fighting in the fog. Harry drew more and more ice into the room until he had formed a solid wall of it, sealing them from the mass of liquid metal spiders that flowed and splattered angrily against his barrier as they tried to bludgeon their way through it.

Penny dropped to her knees and scooped up a handful of the nanite dust. "Come on, Cain, give me something."

"Who's Cain?" Burleigh asked, sides heaving. He had cuts on his face and arms.

"My assistant," Penny said. "And she's being a pain in the ass right now. You're not hurt that bad, Cain. Mars was worse than this."

"You've been to Mars?" Harry gaped at her.

"Later," Penny retorted. "Start making a tunnel upward from here. Forty-five degrees that way." Her cannon swiveled to point in the indicated direction, and if that weren't enough impetus, she blew a hole in the wall with it. "Ocean is that way, about seventy meters. It's mostly dirty ice between here and there."

"I can work with that," Harry said, and began reshaping the ice around the hole, widening it and pushing it further and further back. "What are you going to do about the rest of this place? I don't know how much more of that liquid metal they've got."

"I'm trying to address that now," Penny said. "Cain, I swear to God, I will fire you and you can spend the rest of your life in a thumb drive!"

Energy crackled around her hand holding the glittering dust. It seemed to melt back into liquid and flowed around her. The powder on the floor liquefied and swirled around Penny's legs. "What do we do?" Burleigh asked.

Penny held up her hands. Her armor was changing, silvery spirals and patterns mixing into the blue metal. "Nothing. She did it."

"Did what?" Maia asked.

"Hacked the alien tech. I can control it now." The drifting dust drew itself into Penny, adding to her mass until her armor was massive, perhaps twice its previous size.

"How can you even move?" Harry asked over his shoulder as he continued boring a hole upward toward where Penny said the ocean was.

"I don't have to do anything. The suit is doing all the hard work. I could dance a jig right now . . . if I could dance."

"Anybody can dance," Burleigh said. "'Cept, you know, white folks." He grinned and Harry laughed. "What's next?"

"Next we blow this popsicle stand and go home."

Chapter Twenty-Six

From Maia's playlist: "Long Walk Home" - <u>Bruce Springsteen</u>

They split up, which Maia just knew was going to go wrong. Burleigh stayed with Harry, keeping watch and ready to defend the ice-controlling hero as he bored his way toward the ocean. Penny brought Maia with her as they headed deeper into the base to find and destroy the main power supply and data core. At first, Maia was excited to have such a powerful ally with her, but then she realized she was probably the biggest liability in the group, and Penny was keeping a close eye on her. That tempered her enthusiasm.

None of the metal spiders awaited them as they emerged into the hall. Any residual liquid metal flowed into Penny to mix into her armor. "How long can you keep that up?" Maia asked her.

"Long as I need to. Individually, nanites are not complex devices. When you can override their fundamental programming, you're in charge."

"You sound more like a scientist than a sniper, yeah?"

Penny chuckled. "Over the years, I guess I've picked up a little knowledge here and there. It's hard to be immersed in this stuff and not learn something. I'm not an expert by any means. I've got a lot of help. March and the others, and Harlan Washington's data archives, and Cain."

"That's like your Siri, yeah?"

"Huh. That's as good a description as any."

"So what do you want me to do now?" Maia looked around at the empty tunnel, wondering when Tlalit was going to show his face, or if he even would.

"Stay with me," Penny said. "It's important that I don't do things like this by myself. I need to have a partner so I don't do anything . . . impetuous."

"I . . . don't understand."

Penny rolled her helmet back to reveal her face. Her skin seemed drawn tight, as if her armor used her physical body to power itself. "When you're as powerful as I am, it's easy to think of yourself as an island. To go off and try to handle things without help. To forget what it means to have people who depend upon you. With you here, I'm not going to take a stupid risk because I think I can take it. I've got to look out for you, and that'll make me think twice."

"So I'm just . . . I don't even know what to call it." Maia felt like stamping her foot, like she had no real value except as a potential victim.

"Right now, you're my partner, and that's what I need you to be. You've been down here before. Your experience, even limited, is better than me going in blind. You see anything you think I need to know, tell me. Even if it's something you think should be obvious. Sure, I'm a sniper, but I have my blind spots too. Whoa." This last came as the two women emerged into the large chamber full of tanks and failed hybrids.

Maia shivered. "I hated this place the first time we were here. There are a lot of animals. Even old ones, like sabertooth tigers and dinosaurs, yeah? There's a . . . a woman."

"A human?"

"Maybe." Maia looked around, trying to get her bearings. She thought she recognized a couple of the creatures in their tanks. "I think she's that way. It's pretty, uh, disturbing."

"I don't doubt it." Penny's eyes flicked back and forth as if she were looking at data only she could see.

Perhaps her assistant Cain was projecting it onto her field of vision. "That's the direction we need to go."

"That's where Tlalit was."

"Who?"

"He's like an Inuit or something. I think he's the first successful, um, hybrid."

Penny closed her helmet over her face once more. "Far as I'm concerned, he'll be the last. I'm shutting this place down for good." She raised her hand, palm up, and five devices the size of eggs emerged from it to fly off into the darkness.

"What are those? Some kind of drone?"

"Something like that. They'll scan this chamber and give me a complete 3D representation of it. From that information, I can derive the weakest points and place them appropriately. Then they'll detonate on my signal. There won't be anything left of this place but a stain."

"So we can go now, yeah?"

Penny shook her head. "Not yet. I've still got to disable the power source and wipe the data core. I'm pretty sure they're both that way from the readings I'm getting." She pointed in the direction that Maia thought was where Tlalit's strangely artificial den had been during her previous visit.

"Are you sure we're alone in here?" Maia glanced around, wishing on one hand that she could see further into the darkness but on the other afraid of what she might see in the tanks outside of her field of vision.

"No, but I can't detect any motion besides my drones. If we're being watched, it's by a living statue or a dumb security monitor."

The two women set off down the path lit by the luminescent mineral. There were a lot more gaps of darkness in it than there had been in Maia's previous visit. Perhaps the base was already failing with the damage they'd done to it between their escape and Penny's hacking of the alien nanotech. She knew it couldn't be so simple as for them to just wait it out; nothing was ever that easy.

Penny froze as light appeared in a pentagonal doorway a few dozen meters away. Her cannon tracked slowly but deliberately to point directly at the bright spot.

"That's it, yeah? That's where Tlalit had us come to him before. He's like the . . . caretaker or something."

Penny's helmet reconfigured itself to form a clear visor. Lenses slid into place from the cheek piece, stretching forward like an old-fashioned sea telescope.

"I thought you'd have some kind of fancy super-sensors or something, yeah?" Maia asked.

"I'm a sniper. Sometimes it's just better to see things with my own eyes. That looks like a fireplace."

"He had a fireplace."

"I think that's my target. Come on. Unless you'd rather wait here?"

"Are you kidding? This is the scariest place I've ever been." Maia shivered without the slightest hint of irony.

"Hang in there, kid. We're almost done."

Being called *kid* reminded Maia of Burleigh, and that made her smile.

As they entered Tlalit's den, Maia felt like the muscles in her legs were trying to crawl up her spine. She tried to look in every direction at once but couldn't see anything except the strange, rock imitations of furnishings. "I don't see him," Maia whispered.

"Nothing on my sensors," Penny said. "But that fireplace is what I want. That's a direct line to the central power. I may be able to get into the data core from it too."

"How are you going to do that?"

"I'm going to make my own data port and jack into it. My nanotech has integrated well enough with the alien tech to talk to it. All I need is time, and someone to watch my back." Penny turned her helmeted head to look at Maia. "I don't have another gun for you, but what do you prefer, a sword, axe, spear, or club?"

At first, Maia was going to say *axe*, because of Burleigh, but she realized she didn't have the slightest idea how to use one as a weapon. "Uh, probably a spear.

Stabbing and swinging is about as complicated as I can manage, yeah?"

Penny held out her fist and the silvery liquid metal flowed from her armor, lengthening into a spear as long as Maia was tall. "How's this?"

Maia hesitated before reaching for it. "It's, uh, it's okay."

Penny laughed. "It's fine. There's a chain of my own nanites forming the spine of the spear. They've got the alien tech locked in place. It's the safest I can make it. If you don't want it, that's fine. I don't have anything else I can offer you."

Maia steeled herself and took hold of the spear. It was heavy thanks its metal construction, but not so awkward that she wouldn't be able to swing it with enough force to do some serious damage with it. "Yeah, I think this will be fine."

"Good," Penny said. She turned to the fire and stuck her hand into the flames. Maia squealed in surprise for a moment, but the flames, it turned out, were as fake as everything else in the room. They were some kind of projection. Beyond them she saw a tall column made from the same luminescent mineral that lined the floors and walls of the complex. Penny's armor reconfigured itself, thickening around her hand and extending cables and spines that poked and prodded and pushed their way into the glowing object. "This might take a little while. I wish March was here. He's a lot better at this kind of shit than I am."

"You said he's Destroyer's nephew, yeah? So what does that make you, his girlfriend?"

Penny snorted. "Hardly. I barely knew the man before he went off to get himself killed in an antimatter explosion."

"But he gave you all his tech. He . . . he gave you the Moon. That's like, the most romantic thing ever, yeah?"

Penny shook her head. "That's not how his mind worked. He's—he *was* a sociopath. I don't think he was capable of human emotions. Have you ever read about his life? At least, what's in his file?"

"Why would I ever read his file?" Maia asked. "I was, like, eleven when all that happened."

"They don't teach about him at the Academy?"

"Just a bit in Parahuman History. Tornado's funeral. Nicaragua? No, Guatemala. I'm pretty sure it was Guatemala, yeah?"

"Kids these days . . ." Penny chuckled. "Get off my lawn."

Maia wasn't willing to let it go so easily. Having someone to talk to and something mundane to talk about made the secret underground alien base a little less terrifying. "Still, he gave you everything he ever made, yeah? That's not something a sociopath does . . . is it?"

"I don't know, kid. I try not to think about it too much. I . . . I don't want to miss him when I didn't even really know him." She paused. "Wait, something's wrong."

The words sent a chill racing down Maia's spine. "What is it? What happened?"

"It's the power core. It's increasing its output. I think it's overloading."

"You mean, like it's going to explode?"

"Maybe."

"I thought you were going to blow it up yourself, yeah?"

"I was, but this is something else. It's building up to something else. Oh shit!"

"What?"

Penny jammed her other hand against the glowing column, as if by increasing her contact she could accomplish more. "You know how a bullet works?"

Maia shrugged. "They shoot people, yeah?"

"The hammer strikes the primer and sets off the powder, and that explosion drives the bullet. Well, there's something above the power core that looks suspiciously like a payload to me."

"To do what?"

"I don't know, but I'm pretty sure we'll hate it, whatever it is. I suspect it's designed to disperse nanites into the atmosphere. With current polar weather patterns, they could spread across the world in days." Penny's armor flowed like water as her nanites fought their way into the alien system. "I'm going to try to stop it before it goes off."

Something with too many legs and razor-sharp claws dropped onto Penny from the shadows above the fireplace.

Chapter Twenty-Seven

From Maia's playlist: "Shadowplay" - Joy Division

The creature hissed with an ear-searing sound like a pneumatic grinder in a metal shop. Its sudden weight made Penny stagger. "Get it! Kill it!" she shouted. "I can't let go!"

Maia didn't know why Penny was incapable of acting, but it must have had something to do with the way her armor had seemed to flow into the fireplace. Maybe she was tied into the alien systems in such a way that removing herself would have severe or even lethal consequences. Regardless, Maia had to act. She screamed like a banshee and charged in, her spear leveled. The creature roared as the spear struck a glancing blow on its chitinous armor. The blow didn't dislodge it from atop Penny but it scrabbled its claws on her armor, trying to find purchase. Maia recovered from her initial charge and swung the end of the spear like it was a quarterstaff in a Robin Hood epic. The end battered against a long appendage that must have been the thing's neck since it ended in the toothy, petal-like mouth. The metal of the spear clanked against the armor plate protecting the creature's hide and sparks shot away from the impact.

Claws flashed at Maia from awkward directions and one pierced her shoulder, leaving behind a burning puncture wound with blood bubbling from it. Maia screamed and nearly dropped her spear.

"Shit. I'm disengaging," Penny said.

"N-no!" Maia cried. "Finish what you're doing." She pushed past the pain in her arm and lunged at the creature again, putting all her weight behind the strike.

Chitin cracked, and the creature recoiled, losing its footing and tumbling backward onto the stone floor in a jumble of flailing legs. Before Maia could press her advantage, the thing rolled itself sideways and leaped back onto its feet. It charged at her with a peculiar, body-rotating gait that suggested its neck could swivel independent of however its body turned. Its claws chipped bits of rock from the floor as it crouched, then sprang at Maia. Five claws like daggers thrust at her. She planted the spear's butt against the ground and caught the creature on the point, hoisting it into the air. It hissed and flailed, trying to dislodge itself. Suddenly its neck emerged from beneath its body, slimy and wet like it had turned itself inside out. The petal mouth snapped at Maia's fingers. She jerked back, losing her grip on the spear.

The creature yanked the spear right out of its body with a splatter of fluid and tissue. It rolled itself onto its feet and sprang at her. Maia screamed and dodged. A claw sliced across her hip and made her stumble. The creature was on her in an instant, using its clawed legs to pin her arms and legs while the fifth leg hovered over her face. The petal-mouth emerged from the creature's underside once again and snapped at her. The creature wasn't particularly heavy, but the claws were digging into her skin and Maia was terrified of being impaled if she struggled. She tried to call to Penny for help but her mouth had gone completely dry. A bulge appeared in the creature's neck, working down the long tube and making the armor plates spread as it passed. Maia whimpered as the petal-mouth spread open wide and lowered toward her abdomen.

"Hey, asshole . . ."

Maia looked to her left to see Penny standing there, fully armored, cannon lowered at the creature. The creature raised its petal-mouth and hissed at her. With a single chuff that made Maia's ears pop, the cannon fired and the force of it blew the creature off Maia. Whatever Penny had fired at it stuck like a ball of glue. The creature tumbled across the floor and staggered to its feet.

"This is our planet, bitch." Penny's tone was cold as Arctic sea ice. The glue ball exploded into bright white flames, incinerating the creature before it had a chance to do more than take a shaky step.

Maia's heart was racing and her entire body felt like a guitar string wound too tight. Blood oozed from the slice in her hip and ran down her arm. "Th-thanks," she managed. She suddenly felt weak and wondered if she'd been infected when the thing cut through her protective nanotech cover. "I don't—"

The world grayed out.

Maia awakened to find Penny kneeling beside her, gently shaking her awake. "Hey, kid, come on, snap out of it. You're not hurt that bad."

"What—"

"You fainted. I ran a scan. No foreign nanites in your body. You're clean. You'll have a hell of a scar from that puncture but I'm pretty sure you'll be able to play the piano again."

"I can't play the piano."

"You should learn." Penny grinned. "It's never too late to start. I sprayed your cuts down with anesthetic and antibiotics. You're not going to drop dead from the pain or an infection before we get you to some real medical care."

"What about the core thing?"

"I got it, just in time. You bought me the seconds I needed." Penny squeezed her unhurt shoulder. "You may not realize it right now, but you might have just saved the world, Devilfish."

Maia opened her mouth but no words came forth. It was such a . . . *big* idea that she almost couldn't wrap her mind around it.

"I got into the alien data core and corrupted it. If there's a backup somewhere, I couldn't find it. There should be a backup, because that's Data Management 101, but we still don't know how they think. Regardless, this facility can no longer fulfill its original function. Just to be safe, I've got a remote-detonated cannon round attached to the main power generator. When I set it off, this place goes dark."

"So, we're ready to go then, yeah?" Maia's ears popped and she frowned, knowing it meant a sudden pressure change. She was familiar with them from her experiences diving below the waves, but they were underground; sudden pressure changes shouldn't happen unless . . . "Hey, can you reach Burleigh or Harry?"

"I don't know. Let me try. Snowcat, Igloo, this is Sentinel. Come in, over." Penny and Maia waited, but there was no reply. "Snowcat, Igloo, please respond."

Maia's ears popped again. She felt like she was diving, which meant pressure was increasing. "Penny, we've got to get out of here. I think the ocean is coming in. Like, right now."

Penny changed frequencies. "Benjie, are you there? March, respond. Anyone receiving this, please respond."

Maia felt a humid breeze on her face with a tinge of salt to it. "How deep do you think we are below the surface?"

Penny shook her head. "I don't know for sure. Maybe twenty meters?"

"Can your bombs on the tanks seal that room, maybe give us some breathing room?"

"If I blow them and they don't, I'm basically creating a big pile of loose debris to grind us to pieces when it hits here. It'll be like when a flash flood sweeps down a canyon."

"That's probably going to happen anyway, yeah?"

Penny paused, perhaps conferring with her onboard computer Cain. "Yeah, I think you're right. Hang on, I'm blowing them now."

After a second, a series of pops came to Maia on the wake of a growing, growling rumble. "I don't think it helped. I . . . I don't think I can swim out of here. My shoulder's real sore, and I've only got so much air." She found herself surprisingly calm considering her impending death. Was that what it meant to be a hero, to die with one's boots on?

Penny raised her arms and silvery liquid metal flowed from her armor to form a seal over the entrance to the chamber. "That's all the alien nanites I have left," she said. "I don't know if it will be enough, but it might buy us some time. I don't know if I have enough power to burn through twenty meters of solid rock, and every cannon round I fire takes mass away from my armor. I'm already down to forty percent of my nanites. Another ten percent and I won't be able to keep suit integrity."

"What about your blaster thingies? They're just energy, yeah?"

"Yes, but forty percent of my nanites also means I'm low on power."

"Can't you use the alien power? You haven't destroyed it yet."

Penny gaped at her. "Maia, you're a genius!" She shoved one hand back against the fireplace and her armor flowed onto it, creating power conduits, regulators, and capacitors. She used so much of the suit to create her system that the armor disappeared from around her. She looked more like she had a pair of large, ungainly prostheses, one tying her to the fireplace and the other terminating in a sharply curved lens. Her legs quaked under the strain and Maia leaped to help support her. "Jesus, this shit is heavy when I don't have it bracing my skeleton. Shield your eyes, kid. This is going to be ugly."

Maia turned her face away as Penny opened up with her blaster, channeling as much energy through it as she could. Overhead, rock exploded downward as Penny's blaster heated it too fast for it to melt. Scalding hot gravel and sand sprayed over both women, like they were standing in the spark spray of a forge. Maia clenched her teeth against the pain and noise as the blaster dug a tunnel upward. Penny shouted something but Maia couldn't hear it over the din.

Suddenly the metal plug sealing the room's entrance gave way and a torrent of debris rushed into the chamber, borne on ice-cold ocean water. Maia yanked her emergency breather from around her neck and popped it into Penny's mouth as the other woman had no free hands. It wouldn't be much, but it would give her companion a few more minutes of air, and that might be enough to make the difference.

The wave crashed in upon them and Maia braced herself, doing her best to shield Penny from the debris that battered against them. Penny's feet nearly slipped out from under her as the leading edge of filthy water swept across her, but Maia kept her upright. She made herself hyperventilate to store as much oxygen in her body as she could. Almost by rote, she activated the emergency beacon on her thigh. Perhaps its signal would be strong enough for Benjie to find them before they drowned.

The chamber filled with steam as molten rock poured down into the rising water from the tunnel Penny was carving. The barrel of her blaster glowed white-hot, and her face was blistered from the heat. Maia felt like she was getting a terrible sunburn. The flood continued to batter against her and Penny both, with the water level rising past their knees in seconds.

A jet of water shot from the mouth of Penny's tunnel, nearly knocking both women back into the rising current. It took Maia a moment to understand what had happened, and then her heart leaped. "You did it!" she shouted over the rushing water. "There's ocean above us. Can you seal your armor?"

Penny slumped in Maia's arms, eyes shut. The barrel of her blaster dipped into the water, churning it to a sudden boil.

"Penny? Penny?" Maia screamed at her companion, but Penny didn't react. "Penny, come on, you need to seal your armor. Penny, please!" What was the name of the personal assistant? It wasn't Siri. It was something biblical. "Cain!" Maia shouted as she remembered.

"Cain, can you hear me? Cain, Penny's unconscious. You have to seal her armor or she's going to drown." Water rose past her hips, thundering into the room. "Cain, if Penny dies, I think you die too, yeah? Use whatever override you have to. Please, seal her armor!"

Just when Maia was afraid it was a lost cause, blue armor pushed its way through Penny's skin to form a flexible metallic sheath. As it stretched up over Penny's head and face, Maia pulled the compressed air cylinder away from Penny's mouth. She was going to need that air more than her companion. "Thank you, oh thank you," Maia said, feeling like she was on the verge of tears.

The water rose to her chest. She raised Penny, testing to see how heavy the woman was with her armor. She must have weighed several hundred pounds, which would make swimming with her difficult. Maia could lift that much weight easily, but that was when she was braced against a solid surface, not free-swimming. Moving Penny would be more a matter of climbing than swimming, and that meant Maia would burn through her air supply far faster than if she were swimming on her own. She hoped Burleigh and Harry had made it out. The water that came from elsewhere in the base probably meant they'd breached the ocean where they had been.

She would find out soon enough.

The water reached her chin. Maia kept hyperventilating, saturating her system with oxygen. She would have to wait until the water reached the roof and slowed in its cascade down the shaft Penny had created. She looked down at Penny. "I hope that armor's watertight." She let the water rise over her head and watched as it swirled downward, waiting for her chance to ascend.

Chapter Twenty-Eight

From Maia's playlist: "The Ocean" - <u>Led Zeppelin</u>

The first step, as people often said, was a real doozy. Maia discovered right away that she couldn't swim upward with Penny in her arms. The woman weighed too much in her armor. It occurred to Maia that Penny must weigh that much all the time thanks to the copious amount of nanotech in her body. It sounded exhausting for someone who wasn't already genetically super-strong. It gave her a newfound respect for the woman. Still, respect or not, trying to get her up the twenty feet to the hole in the ceiling was proving a difficult challenge. Maia felt the oxygen stored in her lungs slowly but steadily draining away as she cast about for something she could use as a ladder but nothing presented itself as useful.

Finally, in a move borne of desperation, she crouched down as low as she could, holding Penny awkwardly against her chest like a tandem skydiver, and jumped. The resistance of the water was nearly too much for her, but between her leap and subsequent frantic kicking, she managed to get hers and Penny's torsos into the ragged hole the woman's cannon had made. Before she could fall, she wedged herself against the irregular rock walls while keeping a tenuous hold on Penny with her legs. She wished the woman would wake up and take some of the strain off her. She was already starting to see spots and knew she had to take the second breath of air from her tank. In theory, it would give her another half hour of underwater activity, but that theory didn't account for trying to lift several hundred pounds up a narrow shaft.

Maia's wounded shoulder stung with the icy cold of the water, but the pain helped keep her focused. She hit upon the idea that pushing Penny might be easier than pulling her. It would definitely be safer, because if she dropped Penny, she wouldn't be able to lift her a second time. She strained and struggled to pull the woman up past her body without losing her position in the shaft. At one point, she slipped and nearly sent the two of them tumbling back to the floor of the room below, but her fingers caught a sharp piece of denser rock jutting from the wall and she hung from it, holding Penny tight against her. Inch by inch, she pulled herself upward until she could wedge her shoulders and hips against the shaft. Thus braced, she pushed Penny upward and began climbing the shaft while shouldering the heavy woman higher and higher.

The current still pushed against her, but the force was diminished enough that she wasn't afraid of being sucked back downward. Her biggest fear was running out of air before reaching a depth where someone might be able to catch her emergency beacon signal.

Cold light filtered through the water of the shaft, suggesting she might not be too deep below the ocean's surface. It gave her a tiny bit of hope as she struggled to get Penny past an obstruction in the shaft. She had to brace both her legs against the sides of the shaft and twist Penny past the jutting rock. It was hard work, and Maia could feel the oxygen in her system bleeding away with the effort.

One good shove and suddenly Penny flopped sideways. Maia didn't understand for a moment, then nearly gasped with the realization that she had reached the mouth of the shaft. With a few powerful kicks, she pushed herself free from the rough hole to find herself maybe ten meters below the surface. A plain of rough, dark rock spread out around them, patches of murky, soft sediment sitting upon it like ponds on a surface plain. Pale orange-white starfish dotted the surface, moving slowly across their feeding grounds while spiky urchins made their way between or occasionally over the stars. The familiar sight of earthly animals—even the weird undersea ones—in such an alien environment as the Arctic gave Maia a burst of new energy. She turned to check on Penny and the ocean thundered like a giant had struck it with a hammer.

A shockwave tore through the water, blasting the starfish and urchins to bits and sending Maia tumbling head over heels through the water and pushing all the remaining stored air from her lungs. The water filled with debris and bubbles, obscuring her vision. She couldn't see which way was up, couldn't see Penny, and had no air to breathe. She crashed against the rocky ocean floor and felt like she was being battered in all directions. Had the base below exploded?

She tried to swim for the surface but her leg was wedged in rocks that the explosion had dislodged. She pulled hard, feeling her ankle threaten to shatter, but that would have been a small price to pay not to drown. The rocks around her shifted, seeming to flow downward like they were being washed down a drain. She tugged but couldn't get herself freed. Bright spots formed in her vision and her pulse pounded in her ears.

Suddenly the impossible vision of Burleigh appeared before her. It was impossible because he couldn't swim. He'd told Maia so. Still, even as her vision darkened, she felt his hands on her, putting something over her head. It constricted around her neck, but gentle like the elastic band of a sweater instead of a choking attack. Water drained away from around her head and in its place she found sweet, sweet air! She inhaled deeply, filling her lungs and letting the oxygen spread forth to her starved tissues.

Her vision cleared enough to see she had some kid of plastic bag over her head, and something in it was providing air. Surely it was some kind of nanotech.

Burleigh had a similar bag over his own head, and his axe was clutched tight in one hand like a sacred totem. He had a harness over his shoulders with a cable running up toward the surface. "Burleigh!" Maia gasped. "Can you hear me?"

He looked up at her as he used the axe as a lever to pry the gathered rocks away from Maia's leg. "Kind of." His voice was muffled and distorted by the water between them, sounding as he were behind a thick door. "Hold still, kid."

Maia grabbed Burleigh's arm and shook it. "Penny. She's down here somewhere. I lost her in the explosion!"

"She'll be fine."

"No, she's hurt and unconscious. She needs our help, yeah?"

"Maia, trust your teammates. You don't have to do it all yourself." Burleigh used the axe handle as a spacer and got his fingers underneath the big boulder that had trapped Maia. "Get ready to move, kid. On three." Maia nodded. "One . . . two . . . *three!*"

Burleigh raised the rock a couple inches and Maia wrenched her leg free. She felt her costume tearing and gasped at the pain as the rock's razor-sharp edges penetrated her super-tough skin to lacerate her calf. A cloud of blood appeared in the water and she had a completely irrational thought about piranhas. "I'm clear," she called.

"Grab the axe before I let this go," Burleigh said. Maia slid the titanium axe out from under the rock. Burleigh dropped it and it fell back, making another cloud of silt rise from the ocean floor.

Maia held the axe out to Burleigh and once he took it, she threw her arms around him. "Thank you. I was going to die. I was out of air."

Burleigh embraced her as well, then stepped back to look at her. "You're a mess, kid. You look like you came out second best in a fight with a cutlery drawer."

"I'll be okay. How did you find me?"

"Juliet did. She's in the ship with the rest of the team."

"But—"

Burleigh raised his finger to touch the bag over her lips and Maia went silent. "Can you still swim?"

"Yeah, I think so. Why?"

He smiled. "Because I still can't and I'll be damned if I'm going to let them reel me in like a fish."

* * *

Benjie thoroughly exhausted himself in the search for Penny and Maia. When he lost them deep in the underground base, he transmitted himself back to the Preserve for reinforcements. Apparently, when the plight of their teammates became known, Michelle and Tanya refused to be left behind. Michelle, still suffering from the aftereffects of her near-death experience, was taking supplemental oxygen as the Preserve's nanites worked to repair the damage to her lungs. Even so encumbered, she said she could still use her powers, and if she could find the slightest hint of a transmission, she'd be a conduit for Benjie. With the Hind Garragh left to look after the Preserve and Penny's son, the others returned to March's ship and commenced their search.

"How did you guys manage to flood the compound early?" Maia hissed as Harry applied antibiotic cream to the scratches on her thigh. He'd sprayed some kind of numbing foam into the puncture in her shoulder and left her with a maddening itch *inside* the muscle that she couldn't scratch.

Harry blushed. "That was my fault, beginning to end. We were making good progress on the escape tunnel. The spiders had left us alone altogether. Burleigh was keeping watch but with nothing to protect me against, he was pacing and I got . . . distracted."

"You got mad, yeah?"

"Not mad, just . . . distracted." Harry put down the tube of ointment. "I punched through the ocean floor before I was ready. I didn't have enough ice in the tunnel to seal it before we were knee-deep in water. We knew it was only going to get worse so we called for an extraction. Benjie got the two of us out. By then he was going a little crazy because he couldn't find you and Penny."

The search had continued until March had detected an underwater explosion. He'd flown the ship to hover over the area and then Juliet got a psionic ping from Maia. "You know what happened after that," Harry said. "Burleigh wouldn't hear of anybody else going down. The storm was already weakening. By that point, it was mostly just regular choppy seas and wind. Cale lit up as much of the ocean as he could and Burleigh went down to find you while Juliet found Penny. March went into the ocean himself to get her. He's got as much scary nanotech as she does. We got everybody back aboard the ship and then Benjie saved us a long flight home and zapped us all back here. Poor guy's probably going to sleep for a week."

Maia looked around the sickbay of the Preserve. Michelle lay resting on the bed to her left, breathing more easily than she had in hours. According to Harry, she was likely to make a full recovery within a day. "How's Penny?" Maia asked.

Harry shrugged. "Apparently she's going to be fine. She's somewhere here on the base, getting pumped full of fresh nanotech and getting her burns replaced with new skin." He shuddered.

"This nanotech stuff kind of skeeves you out, yeah?"

"Yeah. It's the kind of technology that feels like it's only a heartbeat away from dissolving the whole world into gray goo. And Penny and March are walking around literally with hundreds of pounds of the stuff inside them. It's like they're not even human anymore."

Maia lay back on the bed and stared at the ceiling. "*Human* is how we act, not what we are. Look at me, Harry. I don't look human. I'm like some kind of . . . blubbery hybrid. I'm not any different than those things down in the tanks in that base. I've got human DNA and parahuman DNA and alien DNA all mixed together. And so do you. So do all of us, yeah?"

"That's a simplistic way of looking at it."

"It is, because if we can't define *human* at a—a biological level, we have to do so another way. We love. We laugh. We care about one another. That's what makes us *human*. Maybe what's-his-name, the Hind, he's human too. He cares about others, yeah? He's Penny's friend. He works with her. He cares what happens to her."

"Sounds like you're saying everyone is human. Even aliens." Harry smiled. "You missed your calling. You should be an ambassador to the stars."

Maia laughed, then stopped as she realized that might actually be a real thing now that there were aliens and other stars for which ambassadors would be needed. "No, I couldn't ever do anything like that."

"You might be surprised what you can do, Maia. You're a brilliant young woman and a terrific hero and we are all indebted to you. I can promise you will be commended for your actions today."

"I don't care about that. I just want to get back home."

"Home to your family? Need some time off? I'm sure we can arrange that."

"No, home is Deadhorse, and you guys are my family."

Chapter Twenty-Nine

From Maia's playlist: "Home by the Sea" - <u>Genesis</u>

One of the perks of being a parahuman in the Just Cause organization was the right to leave it at any time. Although its members were compensated for their time and efforts, both financially and with a generous benefit package, nobody was under any contractual obligation to be a superhero. Using one's parahuman abilities for the greater good of one's country and one's world required a very specific and often delicate psychological profile. Ever since the first days of American Justice, the first superhero team after World War II, it was understood that membership was strictly voluntary, and nobody should ever be forced to stay.

So when Penny offered Michelle the chance to join the Preserve and help defend the world in different ways than she had as part of Just Cause, nobody was particularly surprised that she took the offer. She'd wanted out of Just Cause Arctic Circle since her first day on the job, but hadn't ever quite gotten up the nerve to walk away entirely. Penny gave her that chance, and she took it.

"You know it's even colder here on the Moon than it is back in Deadhorse," Burleigh said.

"Yeah, but I don't ever have to be out in it," Michelle said. "Besides, it's quiet up here. You have any idea what it's like to be able to hear radio signals constantly? It's like having headphones on, tuned to every station all the time. I don't know what they did with their nanotech but it's like there's a volume control in my brain. I can turn it all the way down now." Tears came to her eyes and trickled down slowly in the lunar gravity. "It's wonderful."

"We're sorry to see you go," Cale said. "But you always have a place at JCAC if you want. And I hope if we ever need you, we can call on you."

"Of course you can. Someone's always listening up here." Michelle smiled. "It's what we do."

* * *

Penny recovered from her injuries with remarkable speed once her nanotech reserves were replenished. She was able to rejoin the others after only a few hours in the tank. The skin on her arms was shiny, pink, and velvety smooth, like the skin of a newborn. "It'll toughen up soon enough," she said as Maia bent to get a closer look. "That's what happens when you work for a living." She visibly steeled herself and turned to face Maia. "I owe you an apology, Maia."

"For what?"

"I didn't consider what would happen to my failsafes if I went unconscious. I always intended for that charge I put on the power core to be detonated manually. When I went unconscious, it started a timed countdown and I understand that you nearly died when it blew. I can't apologize enough for that. I'd feel awful if you'd died because of my mistake."

"Oh. Uh, it's okay. I mean, we both got out intact and that's what matters, yeah?"

Penny went to her sidebar and poured out a couple of fingers of an amber liquid. "You want one? It's a damn good bourbon."

"Um, I'm only eighteen."

Penny shrugged. "This is my world, my law. You want a drink, have one."

"No thank you."

Penny sipped at the spirits, letting the liquid roll around her mouth before swallowing. "I don't get out in the field as much as I probably should. Before I did this,

I was a tactical specialist for Just Cause New York and before that, a police sniper. I'm used to doing stuff on my own, and even all these years later, I sometimes forget what it means to have a partner in the field. It's not just about me needing to have someone to look after to keep me sharp. It's also about allowing that I can have weaknesses too and having a partner can cover those blind spots. It's why Just Cause teams have a Field Commander and a Second. I've been running on my own for too long and I keep thinking about solving problems *my* way, even though that might not necessarily be the *best* way."

"You've got a team up here," Maia said. "Maybe you need to tell that to them, yeah? Make one of them your second. Even when, uh, Sara died, Cale still made Burleigh his second."

"You're right. I just wish it hadn't taken putting you in danger for me to learn my lesson. I am terribly sorry about it. Please tell me there's something I can do to make it right." Penny looked at her and Maia saw real pain on the woman's face.

"It's okay. I, uh, I forgive you. You saved my butt down there too, you know. We were a pretty good team." Maia smiled. "I know you said you weren't going to, but I hope you don't erase our memories. I kind of want to remember this, yeah?"

"Erase your . . . is *that* what you think we were going to do? Like some kind of brain-zap or something? A bright flash and the next thing you know you're home in bed?" Penny laughed, not unkindly.

Maia felt her face grow hot. "It makes sense. You've got the biggest secret in the world to keep up here."

"Can you keep a secret?" Penny asked.

"Yeah."

"Then I expect we have nothing to worry about." Penny touched a control on the wall and a bulkhead silently slid aside to reveal the stark and beautiful lunar landscape beyond. "I'd hate for you not to remember this sight."

Maia walked over to stand beside her. She could smell the bourbon in Penny's glass, sharp and sweet at the same time. "I'm just glad to know you're up here, watching over us all. The world needs people like you."

Penny turned to look up at her. "Not as much as it needs people like you, Maia. You're a good person, and it has been my privilege to know and fight beside you." She held out her hand and Maia shook it.

"No, it's been mine too, yeah?"

"March is going to fly you back home. No more running back and forth for Benjie for a while. I can't have him too weak to operate if there's an emergency."

"No problem. As nice as it is up here, it'll be good to get back home."

Penny stared out the window. "You could stay, you know. You're sharp. You're honest. And you're a good person, Maia. It would be an honor to have you join me."

Maia gave it serious consideration. She'd enjoyed working alongside Penny and she knew she would learn so much if she said yes. Her life would be full of the amazing and the unexpected. On the other hand, she'd made friends on Just Cause Arctic Circle, too, and she really was the optimal kind of parahuman for that group. She *belonged* there, in a way she'd never belonged anywhere else. "Maybe someday in the future, but not right now. My team needs me. And I guess I kind of need them too, yeah?"

Penny knocked back the rest of her drink. "I understand. Please know that the offer stands open whether it's tomorrow or twenty years from now."

Maia nodded. "Thank you."

"Thank *you*, Maia. Be well, and have a safe flight back home."

Maia turned to leave. Just before she walked through the door, she heard Penny mutter under her breath, "God damn you, Harlan Washington."

* * *

Cale sent Burleigh and Maia to the coastal rigs to survey damage from the storm and to make sure no oil was leaking into the ocean.

At least, that's what Maia told him to say.

Burleigh had bought it and drove the two of them up the road toward the rigs, but when they reached it, Maia suggested he drive a bit further along the coast. He raised an eyebrow but acceded to her request. After a few minutes she said that was fine and he could pull over. He put the truck into Park and looked across the seat at her. "Okay, what's this all about, kid?"

She smiled. "Turn off the engine, Snowcat. I've got to get something from the back, yeah?" She opened the door and got out. A moment later, a mystified expression on his face, Burleigh shut off the motor and emerged. Maia tossed a backpack at him.

"What's this?"

"A wetsuit. Put it on."

Burleigh's eyes narrowed. "Why?"

"Today, I'm going to teach you how to swim."

"Bullshit." Burleigh threw the backpack back at her.

"You want to be the only black lumberjack who can't swim?"

"The only . . . there's more than . . ." Burleigh spluttered, trying and failing to make any meaningful sentence.

Maia tossed him the pack again. "You risked your life to save mine when you couldn't swim. Next time you have to do it, there might not be a handy nanotech ship hovering overhead. Now get into that wetsuit, yeah?"

Burleigh shook his head. "Kid, you're going to be the death of me."

Maia grinned and turned her back to give him some privacy to change. "Not today."

ABOUT THE AUTHOR

Ian Thomas Healy dabbles in many different genres. He's a fourteen-time participant and winner of National Novel Writing Month. He created the popular ongoing superhero series, the *Just Cause Universe*, and is also the creator of the *Writing Better Action Through Cinematic Techniques* workshop, which helps writers to improve their action scenes.

When not writing, which is rare, he enjoys watching hockey, reading comic books (and serious books, too), and living in the great state of Colorado, which he shares with his wife, children, house-pets, and approximately five million other people.

Visit *www.ianthealy.com* for more information.